## Now all they needed was a target

Johnny had guessed the old man would start drinking his windfall as soon as they pushed off from shore, and he might run his gums about screwing a couple of Yankees, but what would it hurt? Unless he was a mercenary mole behind that four-day stubble, gap-toothed smile and dirty overalls, the most he'd do was play up their stupidity to other drunken crackers like himself. He didn't know where they were going, what was in their duffel bags or where they'd parked their ride.

They'd both changed into camouflage fatigues and combat webbing. They donned commo headsets and bandoleers of spare magazines for their long guns and sidearms, buckled on knives and canteens and daubed their faces with greasepaint to lend them the hue of the swamp.

The Bolan brothers were dressed to kill.

# MACK BOLAN ®
## The Executioner

# The Executioner

### Don Pendleton's ®

# INTO THE FIRE

The ORGCRIME Trilogy

BOOK 1

**A GOLD EAGLE BOOK FROM**

# W RLDWIDE ®

TORONTO • NEW YORK • LONDON
AMSTERDAM • PARIS • SYDNEY • HAMBURG
STOCKHOLM • ATHENS • TOKYO • MILAN
MADRID • WARSAW • BUDAPEST • AUCKLAND

First edition July 2004
ISBN 0-373-64308-X

Special thanks and acknowledgment to
Mike Newton for his contribution to this work.

INTO THE FIRE

The consequences of our actions take hold of us quite indifferent to our claim that meanwhile we have "improved."

—Friedrich Nietzsche
1844–1900

Shall I tell you what the real evil is? To cringe to the things that are called evils, to surrender to them our freedom, in defiance of which we ought to face any suffering.

—Seneca
*Letters to Lucilius*
(1st century)

Evil happens. We don't have to seek it out. Given time, it comes looking for us. This time, it's found me, and there'll be hell to pay.

—Mack Bolan

For the passengers and crew members
aboard United Airlines Flight 93.
A hero's rest: 9-11-01

# Prologue

*Coatzacoalcos, Mexico*

It began with the voice.

*"Johnny? Johnny Gray?"*

Not quite, but close enough.

He would remember it, that frozen moment, for eternity—
or the remainder of his life, at least.

"I don't frigging believe it!" The voice rose.

He turned, the tropical sunshine beating down, relentless
even in the shade of his straw hat and despite a fresh breeze
wafting inland from the Bay of Campeche, a hundred yards
due north. For just a heartbeat the street scene seemed to blur,
as he surrendered to the time-slip.

"Brent."

It didn't come out sounding like a question, since there was
no doubt behind it. Schaefer looked the same, allowing for
an extra ten or fifteen pounds—most of it muscle—and the
bleached line of a scar along the left side of his jaw. The scar
was new, since Johnny had seen him last, but it would never
tan to match the rest of Schaefer's rugged face.

"I don't frigging believe it," Schaefer said again. He closed the gap between them with his hand outstretched. It could have been a stainless-steel prosthesis, from the power of his grip.

"Long time," said Johnny Gray.

"Small world," Schaefer replied, grinning.

And getting smaller all the time, Johnny thought. This trip to Mexico was pure vacation, or supposed to be. His last investigation had been tough enough that he'd allowed himself two weeks of R and R, starting at Vera Cruz and working slowly down the coast. Part of the plan had been to get away from everything he knew and recognized; explore new territory, see new sights.

He hadn't been expecting Old Home Week.

"You working?" Schaefer asked him.

"On vacation."

"By yourself?" Schaefer's blue eyes cut left and right, scanning the flow of foot traffic.

"So far," Johnny replied.

"You've got time for a drink, then?"

"Absolutely."

Johnny tried to analyze the tremor of reluctance that he felt, pronounced enough to give his smile an awkward, artificial twist. If Schaefer noticed it, he gave no sign.

They moved together down the sun-bleached sidewalk, Schaefer on the outside, toward the curb. He hadn't lost his military bearing, even in an off-white guayabera shirt and faded jeans, with well-worn Nike runners on his feet. The sandy buzz cut practically dared the sun to roast his brain.

Brent Schaefer was two inches taller than Johnny, and close to thirty pounds heavier. He was pro-football wide through the chest and shoulders, still graceful enough when he moved that Johnny knew the man hadn't lost his edge. It made Johnny wonder where and how he'd gained the new

scar on his face—and if the person who'd marked him survived.

"That place okay?" Schaefer asked, thumb cocked toward
the far side of the street.

The small cantina had a name—Rosita's—painted on the
stucco wall out front. The paint had once been red, Johnny
supposed, but sun and salt-sea air had faded it to washed-out
pink. The door was stout oak, with tarnished brass hardware.

"Looks fine," Johnny said.

They watched for a break in traffic, Johnny counting as
many bicycles as cars on the street. Most of the latter were
old models with urban-camou paint jobs, primer patchwork
over their faded original colors. Crossing in the middle of the
block, they didn't linger to tempt the local drivers with a stationary gringo target.

Rosita's was dark and smoky inside, a jukebox flashing
neon colors in the northwest corner of a large, murky room.
The music was Mexican standard, guitars and trumpets, with
a singer who covered three octaves.

They ordered at the bar, Dos Equis beer, and took the bot-
tles to a table at the back, as far from the jukebox as they
could get without invading the men's room. Johnny counted
half a dozen drinkers at the bar, and maybe twice that number scattered among the small tables. No other Anglos in the
place.

He sipped his beer and asked Schaefer, "So, what have you
been up to?"

"This and that. You know."

Gray didn't know, but he could guess. They hadn't kept in
touch since Johnny took his discharge from the Rangers, but
he still heard things. Scuttlebutt had it that Schaefer had gone
mercenary, selling his skills to the highest bidder. He still had
standards, of course—wouldn't contract straight wet work

through magazine ads, for example—but ethics were flexible in the private sector.

"That keep you busy?" Johnny asked.

"I do all right. Between jobs at the moment, though."

"Something will come along," Johnny responded appropriately.

A shadow seemed to pass behind the clear blue eyes. "I heard you studied law," Schaefer said firmly.

Same old grapevine. Johnny nodded. "Some."

"You work for anyone?"

"I'm not associated with a firm. I mostly do investigations."

"PI." Schaefer swallowed another hit of beer. "I heard that, too."

Johnny shifted the focus, asking, "Are you looking for work in Oaxaca?"

Schaefer took his time with the beer, considering his answer. "Standing down a while," he finally said. "The last job wasn't quite as advertised."

Johnny wasn't convinced that he wanted to know the answer, but then decided, what the hell. "Bad trip?"

"It was a disappointment," was the brief reply.

"Better luck next time."

"Maybe. It crossed my mind to try a different angle, maybe hook up with a training program for a while, cut down the wear and tear."

"Makes sense to me," Johnny said. More than chasing half-assed wars around the Third World, anyway.

"There's something I have to finish first," Schaefer went on, "but maybe after, that's the way to go."

Johnny wasn't about to ask if he could help finish that something. He was on vacation, dammit, and the man seated across the table from him wasn't really dropping hints. In fact, the last comment had sounded more like Schaefer was talking to himself.

There were no debts between them, anyway, which was a blessing. They'd seen action together in the same Ranger unit. But there'd been no special bond between them, once they set aside the near-death experience that was shared among all combat veterans. Schaefer had not saved Johnny's life, or vice versa. No baggage there, and no skeletons slouching in closets.

Above all, there was no reason for Johnny Gray to go shopping for trouble.

No reason at all.

Schaefer was working on it, though. The wheels were turning in his head, chasing a notion that was almost guaranteed to lead them somewhere sticky. Mulling it over, he took another sip of beer, then said, "I don't suppose—"

The street door opened, spilling daylight in a white-hot wedge that cut through the cantina's murk and picked out swirling patterns in the smoky air. The first man through the door was tall and lean, a blacked-out silhouette with the bright sun behind him, the suggestion of unruly hair and some kind of long coat that was definitely out of season in the summer heat. Behind the point man, two more shadow shapes crowded into the barroom.

"You packing?" Schaefer asked.

Terrific. "Not this time."

"My treat, then."

Schaefer tipped over their table with his left hand, dropping to a crouch behind it, while his right hand drew a satin-finish autoloader from beneath the loose peasant shirt. It was either double-action or he had it cocked and locked; Johnny couldn't tell with the glare from the street in his eyes, but the double tap came instantly, with no delaying click-clack from the slide to chamber up a round.

It wasn't like Schaefer to miss at that range, but the point man ducked his first rounds, going low and to the left. Schaefer might've tagged the second guy in line, but Johnny couldn't tell that, either. He was too busy diving for the tavern's filthy floor as all hell broke loose overhead.

The long coats were explained as Schaefer's adversaries unlimbered automatic weapons and began to hose the room. Better to sweat than walk around the streets of Coatzacoalcos with military hardware showing on a shoulder sling. The police might be sleepy and easy to bribe, but they'd still feel obliged to challenge a hit team in broad daylight.

A hit team, dammit!

Schaefer returned fire, but there was no matching the two or three full-auto weapons ranged against him. Cries of pain from the bar and other areas of the room told Johnny the shooters were firing indiscriminately, and it crossed his mind that that might save his life. Massed fire would've shredded their table by now, instead of chipping bits and pieces from around the edges while Schaefer ducked out and back, seeking targets.

Johnny had spotted the cantina's rear exit as they entered, force of habit kicking in. He started crawling for it now, nose wrinkled at the smell that wafted off the floor. If it stinks, I'm alive, he decided, digging harder with knees and elbows to pour on the speed. Behind him, Schaefer squeezed off two more shots, and then Johnny heard him following, letting the other side burn up its ammo on nothing, taking the table and cheap chairs apart.

They had to pass the men's room, and a customer Johnny hadn't seen before chose that moment to open the door, stepping out. He was either drunk or stupid, maybe a mixture of both. A burst of autofire met him on the threshold and punched him back through the doorway, airborne en route toward impact with a urinal.

Keep going!

The hallway past the crapper gave them some cover, but it was only marginally better. The shooters wouldn't have to travel more than ten or fifteen feet to bring the hallway under raking fire. And when he hit the back door running, Johnny knew the sudden blaze of daylight would frame him as clearly as it had the gunmen when they entered from the street.

One problem at a time.

He had to reach the door alive, before it posed a danger to him. If the shooters spotted him and found their range before that, Johnny wouldn't have to think about it twice.

Schaefer was coming up behind him, close enough that his forearm nudged Johnny's foot. Johnny swallowed the impulse to make some remark, aware that any extra noise, however small, would only help his enemies. They were quiet at the moment, either reloading or seeking new targets, and he pictured them advancing through the cordite-and-tobacco fog, kicking bodies along the way to see if they'd nailed the right man.

Take your time, Johnny thought. Haste makes waste.

Ten feet to the back door, and he would have to stand when he got there, no two ways about it. The only way to run out on a firefight was to run. If he tried crawling into the alley back there, he'd be dead before he cleared the doorway.

Rise and shine. Three long strides and out, if none of the shooters was quick enough to drop him on the threshold. Let Schaefer take care of himself. Survival was Johnny's first priority, particularly when he was unarmed and didn't know the enemy or why in hell the three of them were working overtime to kill him.

Do it!

Johnny pushed off from the floor and charged the exit, shoulders hunched, expecting the impact of hot rounds to sting him any second and bring him tumbling down. Instead, he reached the door and hit it with his shoulder, fumbling briefly with the knob until it gave and let him pass.

Johnny hit the alley running, sliding on gravel as he ducked to the left, putting the cantina's back wall between himself and the gunners. None too soon as they cut loose again from the barroom, bullets swarming through the open door like angry hornets. Johnny checked both ways along the alley. It was open at both ends, meaning he wouldn't have to pass the door again when he took off.

Take off, already!

But he didn't. Something made him hesitate, a flashback to his days in uniform when it was a point of duty and honor to leave no comrade behind. Unarmed, he couldn't hold the shooters at bay while Schaefer escaped, but he could wait a few more seconds in the alley. He could do that much, at least.

As if in answer to his unspoken thought, Schaefer burst through the doorway, spinning to fire at his enemies—three quick rounds before the pistol's slide locked open on an empty chamber.

"Shit!"

The expletive was punctuated by a slapping sound that Johnny recognized, even as Schaefer staggered from the hit. He stayed on his feet, spinning through a not-quite-graceful pirouette to clear the open door and rob the shooters of their target. Johnny saw the bloodstain spreading on Schaefer's shirt, beneath the left sleeve, as the man dumped the pistol's empty magazine and fished a new one from his pocket.

"Time to split," Schaefer said, and ran toward the nearer junction of alley and street.

Johnny followed, catching up. "Who the hell are those guys?" he demanded.

"You don't want to know."

"Do I have a damn choice?"

Schaefer flashed him a pain-twisted smile. "Ask again in an hour, if we're still alive."

Thanks for nothing, Johnny thought.

They ran as if their lives depended on it, which was very much the case. The alley simmered, overflowing garbage cans giving off a reek of pure corruption as their contents baked and putrefied. It wasn't quite the smell of death Johnny remembered from the battlefield, but close enough.

Schaefer's parting shots had slowed the hit team enough to let him and Johnny reach the street in safety. Johnny glanced back as they exited the alley and saw no trace of the hunters rushing out behind them.

If they don't know which way we ran—

But would they know if they were watching shadows flicker past the open doorway? Had their eyes and minds been clear enough to note that Johnny and Schaefer had turned to the left, westward, as they fled the cantina? If so, the hunters knew where to look, and only speed would save their quarry now. If not...

There was no time to wait to see what would happen next. Johnny followed Schaefer north along the sidewalk, brushing past oblivious pedestrians and putting half a block behind them at a run before he realized they hadn't been so very clever, after all.

The plug car was a Jeep Cherokee, shiny black underneath a fine layer of beige dust, windows tinted nearly as dark as the paint job. It was waiting at the curb across the street, and roared to life as Johnny and his wounded comrade cleared the alley's mouth. That much was normal, but the screech of rubber as it skidded through a tight U-turn alerted Johnny to pursuit.

Schaefer stopped dead and swung around to face the Jeep

as it approached them from behind. Pain shivered through him as he raised his pistol in a two-handed Weaver grip, but he held it and squeezed off two shots that put holes in the Cherokee's tinted windshield, driver's side. The Jeep lurched and veered hard to the right, jumping the curb to collide with a heavy litter barrel.

"Go!" Schaefer snapped at him. "Go!"

"You, too."

"Give me a second. I'll be right behind you."

An argument could get them both killed. Johnny ran.

Behind him, he heard men shouting in Spanish and English, and at least two women screaming in the universal language of fear. He didn't hear doors open on the Cherokee or pick up any conversation from its occupants, but there was no question of missing Schaefer's contribution when his pistol popped off three more rounds. Another crash of glass, and Johnny glanced back long enough to see the wounded soldier loping after him, head down, running on sheer determination.

And he wondered whether it would be enough.

More automatic weapons opened up behind them, the staccato reports eclipsing cries from frightened locals and tourists. Johnny saw his opening and ducked into a shop that seemed to specialize in plaster busts of Nefertiti and Elvis. He wasn't sure how either one related to Mexican culture, and there was no time to think about it now. Schaefer was on his heels as Johnny entered the shop, but their evasive maneuver had been duly noted.

They were halfway to the shop's back room when someone shot out the large front window, raking the shop with automatic fire. Inscrutable Egyptian faces shattered into dust; the King likewise, exploding as if so much talent couldn't be contained within a finite shell.

Schaefer grunted and hit the vinyl floor, facedown. Johnny broke toward a showcase on his left and threw himself across it in a shallow dive, landing almost in the startled proprietor's lap. Johnny hit the floor rolling and collided with the smaller man's legs, taking him down. His Spanish was good enough to follow the rapid-fire stream of invective pouring from his unwilling host's lips, colorful to say the least, and he saw the move coming when the Mexican made a lunge for the showcase.

A sawed-off double-barreled shotgun hung beneath the cash register on hooks made from old wire coat hangers. Johnny intercepted the proprietor halfway to the gun and cracked him with a flying elbow that put him to sleep. The scattergun snagged on its hooks, first try, but then he had it down and in his hands.

It was a virtual antique with external hammers, like something a stagecoach guard would carry in an old John Wayne movie. The side-by-side barrels were cut down to fifteen inches or so, the stock truncated and taped for a crude pistol grip. Johnny broke the gun to make sure it was loaded, before he committed himself, then snapped it shut again and thumbed back both hammers.

Schaefer had recovered enough to return fire, lying prone behind a rack of fringed leather jackets that offered concealment but no real cover. Two gunners were edging into the shop when Johnny rose behind the showcase counter on their left, sighting down the shotgun's stubby barrels.

He took the first one by surprise, stroking the shotgun's forward trigger and riding the recoil as it peppered the gunman with a storm of pellets. One blast revealed the fallacy of using a sawed-off 12-gauge to defend a pottery shop, but it took down his adversary without a whimper, flattened in a spreading pool of blood.

The second shooter was recoiling as Johnny swung around to face him. He had a submachine gun, some kind of bargain Uzi knockoff. He held it like a man who knew his weapons cradled a familiar piece. Startled but not exactly frightened yet, the shooter pivoted to face his unexpected enemy, already firing as he turned.

Schaefer hit him from the floor with a clean shot, angled upward. It might have been enough to do the job, but Johnny fired his second barrel anyway and blew the shooter back toward the sidewalk in a spray of window glass. He hit the pavement rolling and ended facedown in the gutter, his body covering his weapon.

Johnny spent a precious moment searching in vain for spare cartridges, then dropped the useless shotgun and stepped around the showcase, watching the street as he moved toward Brent Schaefer. He didn't know how many gunners were left, or how soon they would dare to rush the shop, but common sense told Johnny that he didn't have much time.

Schaefer was bad. He'd taken two hits in the lower back, along with the wound in his side, and he was losing blood at an alarming rate. When Johnny tried to help him up, Schaefer's legs thrashed uselessly and couldn't hold his weight. Johnny was considering probabilities for a successful fireman's carry, wondering how far he'd get with Schaefer slumped across his shoulder, when the soldier caught his wrist with urgent strength.

"I'm done," he said. "Take this." The pistol's grip was slick with sweat as Schaefer pressed it into Johnny's hand.

"No one gets left behind," Johnny reminded him.

"Screw that. I've broken every rule that counts."

"We've still got time." Not much, but maybe just enough.

"No time," Schaefer corrected him. "Get out of here, before they make your face and hook you up with me."

Johnny checked the door again, counting seconds in his head. Still time, perhaps. "What's it about?" he asked.

"Long story," Schaefer said, fading.

"Give me an abridged version."

Schaefer forced a smile at that. "Too late. There's nothing anyone can do about it now."

"Try me."

"Funny. I wasn't gonna squeal. Just wanted out, you know?"

"Out of what?"

The blue eyes had turned glassy, drifting in and out of focus. "You wait a long time for a decent war."

Some do. "What war is that?"

Time was running down. A crouching figure showed itself outside the shattered door, then ducked back out of sight.

"You'd dig it, brother. Isla de Victoria."

"Man, if we're going—"

"Going nowhere fast," Schaefer said as he stiffened, riding on a swell of pain. "You need to watch yourself. Those fuckers at Bayou LaFourche…"

The hunched form in the doorway had returned, aiming a weapon. Johnny shot him in the forehead and the guy slumped backward, sprawling on the sidewalk.

When he glanced back at Schaefer, there was nothing left behind the eyes but emptiness. And Johnny Gray was definitely out of time now, if he planned on getting through the afternoon alive.

Too late already?

Maybe not.

He left the shop's proprietor unconscious behind the counter and ducked out through the back, into another stinking alley. There was shade, but not enough to break the heat, much less offer concealment from determined hunters.

Johnny delayed his flight long enough to grab the nearest trash can and drag it to a point where it blocked the shop's back door.

Not much, but a second gained was crucial now.

Again, he ran. It didn't go against the grain or wound his sense of pride. If Schaefer had still been alive it would've been a different story, but there was nothing more Johnny could do.

As he reached the north end of the alley, Johnny pulled his shirttail out and tucked the pistol out of sight beneath it. He could reach the weapon there, but wouldn't draw unwelcome notice brandishing a weapon on the public street. His shoes had blood on them, but mostly on the soles, and most of that was left behind him in the alley. Rusty-colored traces showed on his jeans, but that could be anything. Who wasted time staring at a gringo tourist's legs, anyway?

Maybe the khaki-clad policeman coming toward him, ambling down the sidewalk with an overstuffed taco in one hand and a bottle of beer in the other. Johnny looked past the cop, like everyone else, giving him the standard urban version of the thousand-yard stare. Eye contact meant guilt to policemen, one way or another. Hold it too long, and the stare implied hostility, perhaps a threat; break it off too quickly, and it was a sure sign of someone with something to hide.

The cop passed him by, more concerned with lunch than unkempt visitors from the north. Johnny was twenty yards past him and starting to unwind a little when he heard shouting behind him and a bottle cracking on the sidewalk.

He glanced back the way he had come, conforming to the crowd mentality that way, and saw the policeman reaching for his service pistol, standing in a pool of beer with taco fixings on the side. Two shooters armed with automatic weapons had come from the alley, surprised to meet a cop first thing, before they could eyeball their quarry.

Stand and fight, or move on?

Wisdom told him to go with the herd, make himself as inconspicuous as possible. That meant running for cover—or just plain running—as the patrolman drew his weapon and the gunners opened fire in reflex, spraying the sidewalk with bullets.

As such things went, it wasn't much of a firefight. The Mexican cop was outnumbered, outgunned and outclassed. Whatever training and experience he had hadn't prepared him for hell at high noon. He got off one .38-caliber round as the gunmen cut loose, missed with that one and squeezed off one more as he fell, dead or dying before the concrete rose to meet him.

Johnny ran, head down, shoulders hunched, with one hand on the weapon tucked in his waistband. It made running awkward, made his jeans pinch him, but Johnny ignored it. People rushed around him, helter-skelter, some of them colliding with him like human pinballs. He shouldered them away and looked for cover on a street that offered little in the way of protection from automatic fire.

Had the shooters seen him? Would they know him if they had? The three men he'd faced in the pottery shop were dead now, or the next thing to it. Johnny didn't know if the gunners from Rosita's were back in the chase, or whether they'd seen enough of him to pick him out of a crowd, but common sense told him to get off the street as soon as possible and find a shortcut back to his hotel.

Another alley opened on his right, and Johnny ducked in there. He wasn't alone, by any means, but most of the dozen or so people hiding there had gone to ground, using the nearest wall or garbage bin for cover. Johnny kept going, pouring on the speed now that he wouldn't stand out as a running target in the shooters' eyes.

Behind him, from the street, short bursts of automatic fire told Johnny that his pursuers were scattering stragglers, either cutting them down or firing into the air as an added incentive to run. He didn't know how quickly police responded to a shooting call in Coatzacoalcos, but he hoped they were equal to the challenge when they finally arrived.

In the meantime, he was busy making tracks.

Fifteen minutes later, after winding in and out of narrow streets that led him south and east toward his hotel and the rental car he'd abandoned that morning in favor of touring on foot, Johnny reckoned he was in the clear. There was still an outside chance he'd meet the shooters cruising, and that one of them would recognize his face. But the odds were so remote that he felt safe in discounting them. Add that to the converging sirens north and west of him, and Johnny guessed the hunters would be fleeing now, debating ways to break the news that they'd completed only half their job.

Strike that.

They'd come for Brent Schaefer, and that job was done. Johnny Gray was something else, an unknown quantity, and they'd have to think about it for a while, asking themselves if Schaefer had spilled the proverbial beans.

But had he?

Isla de Victoria. Bayou LaFourche.

What the hell was that about?

Two blocks from his hotel, Johnny slipped into another of the town's innumerable alleys, wiped the pistol with his shirt-tail and dropped it into a half-filled garbage bin. After tucking in his shirt and wiping his sweaty face with a clean handkerchief, he continued the trek to his lodgings.

Two nights remained on his scheduled reservation, and Johnny knew the best way to draw unwelcome attention would be to check out ahead of time, rush off to the airport and exchange his tickets for an earlier flight. If watchers were waiting, even if they didn't know his face, such erratic behavior would sound the alarm.

Play it cool. See it through.

There was no rush now, at least on Brent Schaefer's behalf. As for the rest...

Isla de Victoria?

It didn't ring even the faintest bell of memory.

Bayou LaFourche?

He'd never heard of it. But someone had.

The trick lay in asking the right questions of the right person—and living to process the response.

**1**

*Tucson, Arizona*

This time he was prepared. He couldn't guarantee there would be no surprises at the meet, but Johnny Gray had taken every possible precaution. Tucson was a neutral city, far enough from San Diego that he wouldn't jeopardize his own home base if anything went wrong, laid-back enough that a tail should be easy to spot, spread out enough to give a man some combat stretch if fighting was required.

He had driven from San Diego a day in advance of the meet, four hundred miles along Interstate 8, watching his rearview and stopping when the spirit moved him, taking short detours, making sure he wasn't followed. Prior to rolling out he'd checked the Blazer carefully for any trace of bugs, homing devices and the like. It had been clean. Johnny hadn't felt the least bit foolish for going the extra mile with his security precautions. It was the best way that he knew to stay alive.

Even then, survival wasn't guaranteed.

There'd been no problem getting out of Mexico. No flight delays or unusual questions at customs. He'd been alert for watchers, knew he might have missed some, but if any were in place around the Coatzacoalcos airport they'd been first-rate chameleons and made no move to tip their hand. His flight was nonstop into Houston with ninety minutes on the ground before his connecting flight to San Diego started to board. That had given Johnny time to find an overpriced café and watch the human sideshow that was more or less the same in every American airport.

Once again, if anyone was tracking him, he couldn't pick them out.

By the time he landed in San Diego, ransomed his wheels from licensed extortionists in long-term parking and made his way home, Johnny felt confident that he had pulled off his exit without a hitch. There'd been no unauthorized entry to his apartment, and a thorough sweep of the flat revealed no electronic surveillance in place besides his own.

Why should there be?

He'd had a close call in Coatzacoalcos, granted, but the shooters had clearly been gunning for Schaefer, not Johnny Gray. They might have glimpsed his face in Rosita's or fleeing the scene, but so what? There'd been nothing to identify him, no pointers to give a hunting party directions. Six days since the killing in Coatzacoalcos, and no one appeared to be tracking him yet.

Smart money said he was clear.

So, why was he stepping back into the shit?

Brent Schaefer was part of it. Even if they hadn't been the closest friends while still in uniform, even though Johnny and Schaefer had pursued divergent lifestyles after discharge from the service, they had still been comrades once upon a time. They'd witnessed death together and inflicted some, had friends in common who were never coming home.

It added up.

Schaefer's death was part of it, but only part. His dying words had cinched it, though. You wait a long time for a decent war. Isla de Victoria. Bayou LaFourche.

He'd run an Internet search on the names and discovered that Isla de Victoria was a former British protectorate in the Caribbean, roughly equidistant between Puerto Rico and Bonaire in the Netherlands Antilles. Granted full independence in the mid-1990s, the island's people had elected their first president—one Grover Halsey—and proceeded to grapple with the same socioeconomic problems that plagued every other tropical nation in the Western hemisphere. Rumors of insurgency had blossomed into verified guerrilla warfare some eighteen months earlier, but the Halsey regime was still hanging on, buttressed by economic and military aid from England.

It would be no great surprise if Schaefer had attached himself to the cause that boosters called the Victorian Liberation Movement, but why had he split from the group? And more to the point, why had a hit team tracked him to his very public death in Mexico? Who had he angered, or what secrets did he carry with him, to make the hunters risk that kind of exposure?

And what was the link to Bayou LaFourche?

That one had taken more digging, but Johnny had finally pinned it down to Louisiana's Iberville Parish, southwest of the state capital at Baton Rouge. He'd found the one-and-only Internet mention of Bayou LaFourche on a website devoted to Kennedy assassination conspiracy theories. If he could trust the site's reportage, Bayou LaFourche had sheltered a Cuban exile training camp in the early 1960s, part of the CIA's covert war against Fidel Castro. The FBI had shut it down on Bobby Kennedy's orders, six months before the guns went off in Dallas, and thereby hung an unprovable theory of cause and effect, with killer chickens coming home to roost.

But how did any of that ancient history—assuming it was even true—relate to a Caribbean guerrilla action in the twenty-first century?

Johnny didn't have a clue.

And that fact, more than anything else, had brought him to Tucson.

Not Tucson per se, of course. That had been a personal selection, derived in equal parts from logistics and convenience. He could as easily have chosen Denver, Salt Lake City, or Las Vegas. Anywhere, in fact, where a casual meeting would pass unnoticed, unremarked.

Because he needed help, and something told him time was short.

Johnny trusted his gut and resented it at the same time. It was no pleasure being distracted from life's daily business, however mundane, by silent alarms or hunches that sent him rushing off into harm's way. Still, there were others who had it much worse; Johnny knew that from personal experience.

He was meeting one of them in Tucson today.

Johnny left his hotel after breakfast, passing maids with their housekeeping carts in the hall as he made his way to the elevator and down to the street. He checked the lobby and found no one idling conspicuously. Tourists always had somewhere to go and something to see. No one in the lobby or out on the sidewalk gave Johnny a second glance.

Perfect.

He parked the Blazer and walked three blocks to Old Town, gazing at the display windows of shops that wouldn't open for another thirty minutes, maybe longer. The Old Town shops were big on silver and turquoise, mixing the two whenever they could with "genuine Navajo" jewelry, belt buckles, string ties and the like. Other novelties included paper-weights—tarantulas, scorpions and baby rattlesnakes entombed in clear plastic—along with handwoven Indian blankets and tiny potted cactis. Postcards featured desert landscapes, Indian dancers and the occasional grinning jackelope.

Johnny checked his watch as he dawdled outside a shop devoted to paintings on black velvet. He'd never understood the passion some people felt for that particular art form. Orange-and-red Elvis in concert. Blue-and-green Frankenstein's monster. Bob Marley in shades of violet. John Wayne in red, white and blue.

Ten minutes and counting.

He moved on toward the rendezvous point, a kind of courtyard surrounded on three sides by shops, open to foot traffic on the fourth, with a bubbling fountain in the middle. He had surveyed the meeting place the previous day, after checking into his hotel and catching a shower. He knew the potential hiding places, such as they were, and while he couldn't scan the rooftops from street level, Johnny checked the other danger points and found no lurkers waiting in the wings.

Almost time.

He sat on a bench near the fountain, feeling spray tickle the back of his neck now and then, when the morning breeze shifted. It wouldn't be long, now.

All he had to do was wait.

MACK BOLAN ENJOYED the Southwest. He liked the proverbial wide-open spaces, the vivid colors of red cliffs and mesas, the uncompromising climate. The desert tolerated human beings to a point, but it was not forgiving of careless mistakes.

In that respect, it reflected his life.

Bolan had flown into Phoenix from Chicago, a charter flight with no questions asked about his luggage. He then rented a nondescript sedan and drove down to Tucson on Interstate 10, stopping twice en route to make sure he was clear. No one was tracking him, as far as Bolan knew, but Johnny had been cryptic on the telephone, and common-sense precautions were a normal part of Bolan's life.

In fact, they were the reason he was still alive.

He was between jobs at the moment, a free agent, but his lulls were never much prolonged. He had a window, as it were, and if the problem posed a challenge, something Johnny couldn't handle on his own, Bolan might tackle it.

What else was an older brother for?

They were a different sort of family, the two survivors from a starting group of five, and neither of them used the Bolan name these days. It wasn't healthy, after so much bloody history. Those memories ran deep, and while most of his enemies were long since dead, he'd never profited by tempting Fate.

Johnny Bolan had been Johnny Gray since his teens, the name change formalized by adoption, his court records sealed for all time. As for Mack Bolan himself, he was dead, with The New York Times obit to prove it. Pretty lively for a corpse, as a new crop of adversaries had learned to their ultimate sorrow.

Bolan had cruised into Tucson that morning, early, and used the spare time charting streets and projecting escape routes. It had been a while since he'd passed through Arizona's second city, but his mind retained small details and he didn't need a prolonged refresher course on major landmarks. Old Town was right where he'd left it, with a public car park for the rental and a short walk to the rendezvous.

It was already warm and getting warmer by the moment,

as the sun climbed overhead. One thing about the desert, as opposed to other killing grounds where Bolan had engaged his enemies: it never offered any surplus shade.

He spotted Johnny from a block out, seated by the fountain as agreed. Maybe an ankle holster for a smaller semiauto pistol, since he wore his shirt tucked in and would've looked suspicious in a jacket, even at that hour of the morning. Bolan had compromised, wearing a denim vest over a short-sleeved shirt to hide the Beretta 93-R in its fast-draw shoulder rig, with two spare magazines beneath his right armpit.

He checked out the plaza instinctively, even knowing Johnny would have done so before him. There was no such thing as being too cautious, no cure for negligence when the one and only punishment was death, without appeal. One of the morning shoppers in the plaza was an urban cowboy in full-dress regalia, including a pearl-handled .45 Colt on his hip, but that was nothing unusual for Tucson. Bolan watched the cowboy, laughing with his blond girlfriend, and decided they probably weren't contract shooters.

Not good ones, at least. The pros took care not to stand out in a crowd.

Approaching from the south, Bolan saw his brother turn and smile. He was aging gracefully, a few more worry lines than laugh lines on the handsome face, but in Bolan's mind he would always be "the kid." Some things, God willing, never changed.

Johnny's hand clasp was as firm as ever, a bonding rather than a test of strength. The brothers held it for a double heartbeat, then disengaged, retreating to their own private spaces.

"You look good," Bolan declared. "Nice tan."

"That's Mexico," Johnny replied. "Let's take a walk."

They walked, meandering through Old Town, dawdling here and there to scan the sidewalk or to check reflections in the big shop windows. If either one of them was being tailed, it didn't show. Still, they kept moving while the younger brother told his story.

Better safe than sorry.

Better paranoid than dead.

Bolan absorbed the story, listing questions in his mind but saving them until Johnny had finished. As it was, the telling of it barely took ten minutes. Johnny could've told it on a scrambled phone line or in a coded E-mail, but the Executioner knew why his brother had required the meet.

He wanted to observe Bolan's reaction to the story, pick up on his feel for what had happened down in Coatzacoalcos. There was more to it than an exchange of information or a heads-up on a breaking crisis situation.

Johnny finished as they passed an ice-cream shop, and it was question time. "You hadn't seen Schaefer since your discharge?" Bolan asked.

"Or heard from him," Johnny replied. "We were never that close, in the first place. He went merc after his second tour of duty."

"Looking for trouble and money," said Bolan.

"That's him in a nutshell. It was, anyway."

"You think the meeting was coincidence? An accident?"

"I've played it back a hundred times, at least. No matter how I run it down, it still comes out the same. I really think he was surprised to see me."

"Not an act, then?" Bolan wanted to be sure.

"I can't rule it out absolutely," Johnny said, "but he was never the subtle type. Brent was a hard charger, gung-ho all the way. You'd want him up front for assaulting a bunker, but he'd never be a contender for an acting award."

"You'd bet your life on that?"

"Already did. If he was setting me up for the shooters, I'd

be dead and he'd be sitting in a bar somewhere, drinking his payoff."

"Forget the ambush for now," Bolan suggested. "Is it possible he looked you up specifically to pass information?"

"Doubtful," Johnny answered. "Someone wants to find me, there's the office and apartment. Mexico was only scheduled in the sense of flying down and back. I had no hotel reservations, no travel plans. Just drifting."

"Any chance he followed you from Vera Cruz?"

"Again, it's possible. But if he knew the goons were after him, why wait a week and take a chance on losing me when I drove south?"

"Okay. Call it coincidence. Let's look at motive now. He's walking down the street and unexpectedly spots an old acquaintance. What's going through his mind?"

Johnny considered that as they passed by a Mexican restaurant, delicious aromas wafting from the kitchen to entice them. By the time they reached the music shop next door, he'd run through all the options one more time.

"I'm not sure he was thinking clearly," Johnny said. "I don't know how long he'd been on the run before that afternoon. He spotted a familiar face and took a chance."

"On what?" Bolan prodded.

"Maybe an hour's solace. Small talk. A distraction from his day-to-day. Who knows? If he was looking to confess, he must've overestimated his lead time on the pursuit. We never got past the first block on Memory Lane."

"How did he react when the shooters barged in?"

"Like a trained professional," Johnny replied. "But I know what you mean. He wasn't shocked to see them. Maybe just a bit surprised that they'd found him so soon. Surprised and pissed off."

Bolan switched subjects, telling his brother, "I recall a

briefing paper on Isla de Victoria. It sounded as if the locals couldn't decide whether they wanted to be the next Bahamas or Haiti."

"You're one up on me, then," Johnny admitted. I surfed the Net enough to know the battle is on, but the rebels are still contained. The president, Grover Halsey, has complained to the UN about mercs and 'outside aggressors,' but no one seems to be taking him seriously."

"Maybe they should."

"It makes me wonder," Johnny said. "When was the last time you heard of an indigenous rebel force hiring mercenaries? Particularly white mercenaries. Donations I can understand—money and hardware, absolutely. But mercs on the line doesn't sound much like national liberation to me."

"Maybe you're overstating his role," Bolan suggested. "Schaefer could've been an adviser or trainer. They did that in Sri Lanka and Peru."

"If that's all he was doing, why drop out? Who'd want to kill him for defecting from a classroom?"

No one, Bolan thought. Unless…

"Maybe he saw too much, learned something that he shouldn't have."

"Okay, that tracks. He made a point of telling me he hadn't planned to talk, but only wanted out."

"It makes you wonder."

"Yes, it does," Johnny agreed.

"What would it take to spook him?" Bolan asked.

They paused outside a bookstore, its display window filled with coffee-table volumes of Southwestern photographs and art. Johnny pretended to study the covers while he considered his brother's question.

"Nothing tactical," he said at last. "He wasn't squeamish, anyway."

"Not even with civilian casualties?"

"No." Johnny emphasized it with a head shake. "Not in the normal course of events."

"Something extraordinary, then," Bolan suggested. "What would it take to put him off payday?"

"I wish I knew. Another question's linked to that one— what did Schaefer see or learn that someone else would kill to suppress?"

"Hard to say, without knowing the shooters or whoever pulled their strings," Bolan replied. "What do you know about the trouble on Isla de Victoria?"

"Nothing but broad strokes and slogans," Johnny replied. "It's the usual 'self-determination' line for public consumption, but who knows what's going on beneath the surface? The prez swears he's clean, naturally." Johnny raised two fingers on each hand and slipped into his Nixon imitation. "I am not a crook!"

"Uh-huh. What about the rebels?"

"Nothing I read gave a decent fix on what they stand for," Johnny said. "They want freedom and justice, yada-yada."

"We can run it past Stony Man," Bolan said, "and see what comes out of Bear's computers."

"Sounds like a plan," Johnny concurred.

"The Louisiana angle bothers me, though."

"Me, too."

"Nothing else since the sixties?" Bolan asked.

"Not a word on the Web. I was thinking, though. If the Company used Bayou LaFourche for training on the Castro thing—"

"They might use it again," Bolan finished his thought.

"Somebody might," Johnny said. "The CIA wasn't operating solo in those days. They recruited trainers from the Special Forces and half a dozen right-wing civilian groups, including the Klan and some amateur militia-types."

"The Mob, too, from what I understand," Bolan added.

"New Orleans for sure, and Miami. Of course, they were working with Cubans in those days. Change the race and politics, you stand to lose the old-time sponsors."

Bolan frowned. "The jungle doesn't care. Unless they've turned Bayou LaFourche into a shopping mall since 1963, it still qualifies as a training ground for jungle fighters."

"If they can cover the logistics," Johnny said.

Bolan's frown deepened. Johnny had a point, in that respect. Training foreign troops on U.S. soil without clearance from Washington meant federal prison time for violating neutrality laws and sundry other statutes. Louisiana swampland might make a perfect training ground for jungle combat, but it didn't exist in a vacuum. There would still be personnel and equipment to transport, supplies to purchase, gunfire and explosions to explain. Local police would be the first to pick up rumbles of unusual activity, from fishermen and hunters, birdwatchers and nature hikers, maybe even moonshiners who didn't like troops prowling near their stills. And once the word leaked out…

"Somebody needs to grease the law," Bolan observed.

"Within the parish, anyway," Johnny agreed. "Most likely at the statehouse, too, to cover all their bases."

"That still leaves the Feds."

"Hal ought to have a line on that, or else know where to pick one up," Bolan replied.

"Because, if this is sanctioned by the Bureau or the Company, we could be in a world of hurt."

"I tend to doubt it," Bolan said. "They have their hands full with the Middle East. If they were training anyone right now, it would be someone to oppose Muslim extremists on their own home ground."

"You're thinking private operators, then?"

"I wouldn't rule out an official link, especially if there's money to be made, but we should double-check before we start to look for spooks under the bed."

"Find out what kind of politics this Halsey's pushing, anyway," Johnny replied.

"Seems right."

"I wasn't looking into this," said Johnny, "as a vengeance thing. Just so you know."

"Okay."

"If Schaefer got himself into a jam and had to pay the tab, so be it."

"Fair enough," Bolan said, "if the bill collectors don't come knocking on your door."

"I've played it back," Johnny explained. "I think I'm in the clear."

"So, would you rather let it go?"

Another pause for thought before he said, "Not yet. I need to know what's going on, why Schaefer had to die and someone tried to take me with him."

That made sense, but Bolan recognized the problem with his brother's plan. "You think they've missed you now, but poking into their affairs could make them stop and take a closer look."

"I'll risk it."

"You know what they say about curiosity."

"I'm not a cat," Johnny replied. "And I'm not exactly a civilian, either."

That was true enough. They had shared missions in the past, though Bolan tried to keep the kid's involvement in his own world to a minimum.

"I should talk to Hal," Bolan said.

"Will he help?" Johnny asked.

"He'll give us what he can. Beyond that, if the operation

comes back as officially sanctioned, there won't be much more he can do. If it's not, something tells me he'll want to know more."

"Then we're in," Johnny said.

"Not yet. There could be angles on this thing we haven't thought of yet, and even if Hal backs a move it doesn't mean we'll find what we're looking for."

Smiling, Johnny asked, "Where's that famous optimism?"

"You're mistaking me for someone else," Bolan replied. "I'm a notorious pragmatist. Some might call me a cynic."

"Not without getting their ears boxed," Johnny said. "How soon can you reach out to Hal?"

Bolan glanced at his wristwatch, mentally bridging three time zones. "Thirty minutes ought to put him in the office, give or take. I'll try him on the hour."

"It will take some time for feedback from the Farm, I guess?" Johnny noted.

"It's kept this long," said Bolan. "If there's something major in the works, it will be there tomorrow."

"That's what bothers me."

"We'll get a handle on it, one way or another," Bolan promised him.

"Okay. You have a room in town?"

"A place out on the highway, just in case."

"I'm at the Marriott. Room 519. They should be finished cleaning up by now."

"I'll be in touch."

BOLAN DIDN'T KNOW what he'd learn from Hal about Isla de Victoria or Bayou LaFourche, but whatever it was, he dreaded the idea of Johnny placing his life on the line. He still felt that inbred sense of responsibility for his younger sibling.

One way around that was to lie, of course. He could call

Hal Brognola in Washington and find out what was happening, then craft a tale for Johnny's ears alone that placed the operation out of bounds. The problem was that one lie bred another, and their whole relationship was based on trust, from childhood through the loss of their parents and sister by violence, to the present day.

Breaking that trust, losing that bond, would cost Bolan more in the long run than toughing it out and meeting the grim truth head on.

Besides, he thought, it may not be so bad.

But Bolan wasn't buying that. No way.

Whatever Johnny's one-time friend had stumbled into, it was bad enough for his comrades or bosses to put out a serious contract and seal his lips forever. How long had Schaefer been at large, outside the fold, before the shooters ran him down? That knowledge would've helped Bolan judge the efficiency of his adversaries, but it was beyond his present grasp.

With any luck, Brognola might be able to help him with that information, too, but Bolan wouldn't count on it. There was such a thing as expecting too much, and he knew from experience that he'd have to work for most of what he got on any job, along the way. If it was all open-and-shut, the big Fed wouldn't have needed him in the first place.

Except for the dirty work.

That was the part of his life Bolan tried to keep Johnny away from, but it was too late to start crying over spilt blood. Johnny knew what he did for a living and how it had started. He recognized the need Bolan filled and had taken on the same role himself, more than once.

They were brothers in blood, as well as in soul.

Bolan was glad the dead mercenary hadn't been a close friend of Johnny's, but he still recognized the sense of responsibility that came with watching a one-time comrade die by violence. Johnny would follow that up as far as he could, with or without Bolan's help, so it might as well be with, if he could manage it.

And if he couldn't, what then?

Wait and see.

If it proved that the U.S. government was somehow legitimately involved in the action on Isla de Victoria, Bolan would stand down and refrain from interfering. But he couldn't vouch for Johnny doing likewise.

If the shooters tried again for Johnny, that was something else. Sanctioned or not, they would be borrowing more trouble for themselves than they realized. With or without Washington's stamp of approval, nobody messed with his kid brother.

Blood was thicker than water, and Bolan had spilled enough of it to know that statement was factually true.

If need be, in his brother's defense, he would spill more. An ocean, in fact, if it came to that.

Let's hope it didn't.

In the meantime, Bolan would prepare for war.

**2**

The maids were gone when Johnny got back to his hotel room. He double-locked the door behind him, then checked to see if they'd done anything more than clean the place. The piece of thread he'd draped across his suitcase latch was still in place, and a sweep of the room with the scanner he carried disguised as a personal stereo revealed no electronic listening devices.

Hurry up and wait.

It was the classic gripe of every soldier, going back to who knew when. Most likely, there had been a Latin version of the saying when the Roman legions marched on Gaul, or something similar in Hebrew when the Israelites were marching toward the walls of Jericho. Waiting was SOP and he was used to it by now, but every fighting man had the prerogative to bitch and moan.

Even when there was no one around to listen.

He knew Mack would be careful, reaching out to Hal Brognola and the crew at Stony Man Farm for information. It wasn't worry per se that made him start to pace the hotel room, before he caught himself and sat down on the freshly made bed. Call it concern about the information that would be retrieved, the scope and nature of the task that lay in front of them.

And it would be them, he'd decided, going into it. No matter what his brother had to say about the risk, even if Brognola offered personnel in support, Johnny was following up this mission himself.

Assuming there was a mission to pursue.

What would he do if Brognola's search for information came up empty? Or worse yet, if it came back as a government sanctioned operation by the CIA, DIA, NSA or some other spook outfit from the netherworld of clandestine alphabet soup? How could he resolve Brent Schaefer's death and deal with those responsible if they came with a federal hands-off warning attached?

Johnny decided he'd jump off that cliff when he came to it. There was no point in borrowing trouble, when each new day brought enough of its own. He had already proved there was no such thing as a simple vacation. Now, the best thing he could do was wait calmly while his brother ran down any available leads and reported back on his findings. There'd be time enough to worry then, and to consider options if the road was blocked by No-Go signs from Washington.

Someone was going to be disappointed in that case, thought Johnny Bolan-Gray. Because he wasn't big on giving up. That seemed to be a family trait he couldn't shake.

It had to be something in the blood.

Crossing his legs, Johnny removed the Colt MK IV Series 80 Mustang Plus II autoloader from the leather holster on the inside of his left ankle. The .380-caliber pistol was loaded with hollowpoint rounds for maximum stopping power, the Mustang cocked and locked because Colts were single-action weapons and he didn't want to waste an extra second in a fast-draw situation.

The Colt wasn't his only weapon—another benefit of driving, instead of using a commercial airline—but it was the only one he'd been able to hide on his person while dressing to suit Tucson's weather. Johnny never knew who might be lurking in the background when his brother came to call—or, since Mexico, who might be tracking his own progress, waiting for a chance to eliminate the last gringo witness. He seemed to be clear, but there were no guarantees, and the risk would only increase if he started poking around in Schaefer's business.

Scratch the "if"; make it "when."

He placed the Colt on the nightstand beside him, picked up the remote control and switched on the television. Surfing past the hotel's menu he settled on CNN. The news was frequently depressing, but he kept abreast of it regardless. There was no legitimate excuse for ignorance.

He watched the full slate of "headline" stories, until the talking heads digressed into Wall Street reports and athletics.

There was nothing on the tube from Mexico, and no reason to expect there would be after a full week and counting since Schaefer's death in Coatzacoalcos. American reporters paid little attention to news from Mexico unless it involved crimes along the border, and even then the slaughter often needed double digits to rate national copy.

Johnny couldn't recall a story from Mexico over the past six months. There'd be no reason to mention a U.S. mercenary killed in a small coastal town on the Gulf. If Johnny's memory was accurate, Schaefer had no immediate family, and even if the U.S. consulate in Vera Cruz had been informed of his death, there'd be no reason to beam the story worldwide.

An American merc had been killed while running away from an illegal war. Who wanted that story to play?

Apparently, no one.

Johnny switched off the TV set and put the remote control back on the nightstand, next to his pistol. He leaned against the headboard, closed his eyes and once again pictured the bloody scene in Coatzacoalcos.

Had Schaefer been ready to die?

In the final moments of his life, did he regret his choice to abandon the project, whatever it was?

Was he sorry for involving Johnny, or had Schaefer been too busy fighting for his life to give the matter a second thought?

It hardly mattered now. Schaefer had paid the price for all his choices, good or bad, and there was nothing more he could do. It was Johnny's game now.

Fair enough, Johnny thought, frowning at the empty hotel room. Bring it on.

*Washington, D.C.*

HAL BROGNOLA RECOGNIZED the trilling of his private line. It was a muted but insistent sound that always generated contradictory sensations, even after all this time behind a desk, watching the world go past on Pennsylvania Avenue. One feeling was a bright spark of excitement, from the old days when he used to roll on calls himself.

The other feeling was a sense of dread.

The private line was special, his direct link to the world outside, unfiltered through switchboards, secretaries and automatic recording devices. No more than twenty people on the planet had the number for Brognola's private line.

A call on the "black line" meant action.

And eight times out of ten, it meant bad news.

Brognola picked up on the second ring, hoping that no one close to him had been reported dead or missing.

"It's me," the deep, familiar voice informed him.

"Hang on," Brognola said. "I'll scramble." He pressed a button on the bulky telephone and waited half a heartbeat, while the small light set beside that button switched from red to green. "All clear on your end?"

"Perfect."

"Glad to hear it," Brognola said. "How's the kid?"

Bolan touched base with the big Fed or Stony Man when he was on the move, left contact numbers, warned the home team when he would be out of touch and for how long. Brognola knew Bolan was meeting with his brother, and the printout on his Caller ID showed a 520 area code, which placed Bolan somewhere in Arizona.

"He's got a problem that needs looking into," Bolan said. Of course. What else?

Brognola frowned and asked, "What can I do to help?"

Bolan laid out the story.

"That's it?" Brognola asked when Bolan finished.

"I'm afraid so."

"Well, it isn't much. Nothing occurs to me, right off the top," Brognola said. "I know they're having trouble on this Isla de Victoria, and have been nearly from the day the Brits pulled out. The Farm can probably supply more information than you want or need, on that end, but I wouldn't count on anything specific to this Schaefer character."

"I'll take what I can get," Bolan replied.

"On the Louisiana end, I don't know what to tell you. We can put it through the mill and see if anything comes up, but right now I'm drawing a blank."

"It has a history," Bolan explained. "From what I hear, the Company trained Cuban exiles in the neighborhood, back in the bad old days."

Brongola's frown felt set in stone. "Okay," he said. "That's something we can check, at least. Land records for a start, to see if we can track whoever owns the property. If it turns out to be some kind of park or refuge, like so many of the swamps down south, we may be out of luck. I can remember Contras and some other nasties training in the Everglades some years ago. Misusing public land is one of the oldest stories in the book."

"I read somewhere there was a Mob connection in the sixties," Bolan said. "The training camps and all, I mean."

"That's true," Brognola acknowledged. "The Mafia and the Company were in bed together on Cuba and who knows what else. Big business, too, for that matter. Castro shut down the casinos and brothels, nationalized the plantations and whatnot. He pissed off everybody. Half the shooters sent in to take him were wise guys from Chicago or Miami."

"For all the good it did," Bolan added.

"Did anybody learn from the mistake?"

"Who knows? With that crowd, some of them seem to think that dedication to a failed idea is proof of loyalty to the Stars and Stripes. You never know."

"We'll have to wait and see, then."

"Shouldn't take too long," Brognola said. "Tonight sometime, with any luck. Maybe tomorrow."

Brognola understood Bolan's reticence to work against the Company. Langley's spook masters were allies, at least in theory, and the White House craved harmony among its diverse servants. Still, the Company sometimes charted courses that placed its agents in direct opposition to Bolan's principles and the goals of the Stony Man team. They had clashed viciously on more than one occasion, and a rogue force had done its best to wipe out Stony Man Farm early on. Bolan's vengeance for that betrayal was still a sore spot in some quarters, but Brognola didn't care. The bastards got what they deserved, in his opinion.

As for this time, though...

"Tonight, maybe tomorrow," Bolan echoed.

"I hope so."

"All right. You have my mobile number."

"Right." It hadn't been a question, but Brognola answered anyway. And he added, "I'll put a rush on it."

"Okay. Thanks for checking."

"No problem." He'd been on the verge of saying, "My pleasure," but they both would've known he was lying. Few of his daily tasks were pleasant, even when they had a happy ending, and rooting around in CIA business was never a barrel of laughs.

"Later, then." Bolan broke the connection without a good-bye, something he'd learned from experience in the hell-grounds, where even soldiers totally devoid of superstition refused to jinx one another with terminal-sounding farewells.

Brognola cradled the black line's receiver, automatically disengaging the scrambler. When he lifted it again, the red light warned him that his conversation wouldn't be in the clear until he thumbed down the button. He tapped out a number from memory, eleven digits, and waited through two rings before a male voice answered him.

"Horizon Farm," it said.

"Brognola, number 317625. Authenticate."

"Authenticated," came the brisk reply.

"I'm scrambling."

"Ready, sir."

The green light told him to proceed. He spoke a name and waited while his call was transferred, keeping salutations brief when Aaron Kurtzman came on the line seconds later. Brognola sketched the story, doling out what little information he possessed. "We need to find the source on this," he said at last, "no matter where it leads."

"No matter where?" Kurtzman repeated.

"We're investigating at the moment," Brognola said. "Operational concerns can wait."

"Okay. I'm on it, Chief."

"ASAP, all right?"

Brognola could've sworn Kurtzman was smiling when he answered, "It's the only way to fly."

## Stony Man Farm, Virginia

THE FIRST PART of the inquiry was simple. Collecting the history of Isla de Victoria required no more than a few computer keystrokes to disclose the information that was found in any almanac.

Christopher Columbus had landed briefly on the island in 1493, naming it Islamorada and leaving enough men behind to guarantee a short life span for the indigenous Arawak people. British explorers claimed and colonized Islamorada 150 years later, establishing sugar plantations and taking their place in the pernicious system known as "triangular trade." Under that system, molasses was shipped to New England and turned into rum, the rum was sent to Africa in trade for slaves, and black captives were sent to Islamorada for "seasoning" on the white-owned sugar plantations. It was a sweet deal for the families on top, until London banned the Atlantic slave trade in 1807 and America's civil war dried up the market a half-century later.

Slavery aside, British masters clung to their colony on Islamorada as they did to Jamaica, the Bahamas, Antigua and other foreign outposts of colonial rule. Generations of bloody conflict were required before the sun at last began to set on the global British Empire, first in Asia, then Africa, and finally across the Western Hemisphere. Islamorada had been reclassified as a British protectorate in 1984, granted full independence a decade later, but the withdrawal of British political leadership—and much capital investment—had produced an atmosphere described by American media anchors in terms ranging from "unrest" to "chaos."

For the past two years or so, Kurtzman learned, guerrilla fighters of the Victorian Liberation Movement had been pushing hard to topple President Grover Halsey's elected government, their efforts producing a volatile climate wherein complaints of atrocities had been validated on both sides. It did not appear that Halsey's regime was in any immediate danger of collapse, but the rebel forces were gaining strength and popular support from the island's impoverished rural majority.

In terms of raw statistics, Isla de Victoria covered 240 square miles, roughly one-third of it arable land. The rest was swamp or jungle, with reports of enough mineral deposits to make the CEOs of certain stateside mining companies pray for an administration more amenable to foreign profiteering.

An estimated two hundred thousand people occupied the island, some ninety percent of them black, forty percent dwelling in the capital at Victoriana on the island's northeast coastline. The dominant language was English; the monetary unit, shared with Antigua and Barbuda, was the East Caribbean dollar. Exports included sugar and certain tropical fruits. The major industries were agriculture, light manufacturing, and—at least before the current troubles—tourism.

Kurtzman saved the stats on his hard drive, made a backup disk, then proceeded to the next phase of his search. The Victorian Liberation Movement was a largely unknown quantity, with little of substance on tap from available CIA files and nothing at all from the FBI's domestic side. An hour of searching told Kurtzman that the movement's leader and self-styled president-in-exile was Maxwell Reed, a forty-something native of Isla de Victoria who had served briefly in the island's parliament before dropping out to go public with claims of corruption and "virtual enslavement" by outside forces. Terrorism charges had been filed against Reed and some of his aides after an April 1997 bombing in Victoriana, and he fled to the U.S. with a plea for political asylum.

Since then, it seemed, Maxwell Reed had done his best to pose as a model of temperance, publicly lamenting the violence in his country while observing that even saints had limited patience, and one man's terrorist was another's freedom fighter. Kurtzman, for his part, was less concerned with rhetoric than reality at the moment, digging as deeply as he could to find the names and political affiliations of Reed's foreign sponsors.

Kurtzman knew those sponsors had to exist. The peasant guerrillas on Isla de Victoria didn't get their weapons from a Cracker Jack box, and they wouldn't come cheap. The only questions left in Kurtzman's mind were Who? and Why?

He hoped that who would not turn out to be the CIA.

A Company bullet had stolen Kurtzman's legs and put him in a wheelchair for life, back when a rogue agent with a messiah complex had taken it upon himself to wipe Stony Man off the clandestine map. That effort had failed, but it wreaked bloody havoc while it lasted and it had left Kurtzman with a deep, abiding mistrust of any and all spooks outside his immediate circle.

Once burned, twice shy.

He didn't want to fight the Company again, particularly since his style of fighting was limited now to chasing leads online and E-mailing reports to Hal Brognola's office at the Department of Justice. Still, there were weapons aplenty onsite, and the shot to his spine had stolen none of Kurtzman's iron will nor the strength in his rock-steady hands.

If the Company had someone else on staff who wanted to pick up where the last crop of losers had dropped the ball, they would find Kurtzman ready and waiting.

His research on Maxwell Reed and the Victorian Liberation Movement produced no apparent CIA links, thankfully, but it did turn up certain other associations that peaked Kurtzman's curiosity. He dug deeper, more determined than ever to get at the truth. Its beating heart eluded him, but he began, slowly, to glimpse the outlines of a picture that disturbed him.

And he filed the details—in his mind, on hard disk, on a backup disk.

Bayou LaFourche was a bit trickier. Large-scale topographic maps were easy to find, if not altogether reliable. Swampland was fluid by definition, watercourses and sodden landmasses often shifting with the season, so that exploring a huge swamp could become a frustrated cartographer's lifework. The swamps of Iberville Parish covered roughly one hundred square miles, with five times that much sprawling over most of St. Martin's Parish, to the south. The borderline between parishes—or counties, as it were—was literally written on water, invisible to any traveler without a GPS homing device or surveyor's tools.

Kurtzman assumed that was part of the appeal. The bayou country offered a semblance of tropical rain forest or worse, ideal for rigorous training programs, and its natural isolation also guaranteed a measure of security. Trackless miles of water, quicksand and dangerous wildlife made razor-wire fences unnecessary, but Kurtzman wouldn't rule them out, either, as one approached the camp's perimeter.

Assuming one made it that far, still alive.

Bayou LaFourche was not located in a state or national park, as Brognola had feared. Instead, registered ownership had passed through a series of corporate hands, while no apparent effort was made to drain or improve on the land. At one time or another, Bayou LaFourche had been owned by a Cajun fishing cooperative, a real-estate developer's consortium, a lay branch of the Roman Catholic church and yet another development corporation. In the 1960s, when as Hal had reported, anti-Castro training operations were run in the parish, Bayou LaFourche had belonged to a southern supermarket chain whose chief executive officer, Kurtzman learned, was a front for silent partner Carlos Marcello, boss of the New Orleans Mafia. Marcello, in turn, had been eyebrow-deep in the CIA plots against Cuba.

Bayou LaFourche and its surrounding swampland now belonged to a consortium called Sea Island Developments Limited. Kurtzman didn't know what the company's limitations were, but he set out to discover who the owners were—and who owned them, if there were any players tucked away behind the scenes.

At 9:05 p.m. he found the answer—or a part of it, at any rate—and knew that it was time to reach out for Brognola on his private line.

*Tucson*

BOLAN BROUGHT the story back to Johnny at the Marriott. He called at 9:30 p.m., suggesting that they meet somewhere outside the hotel, but Johnny seemed confident that his room was clean and Bolan decided to trust his brother's judgment.

There was no reason to believe that Johnny had been followed to Tucson. From the way the hitters had performed in Mexico, they should've made a killing move on him by now. Even if they'd been ordered to watch out for contact, that morning would have been their chance to score, taking out two targets for the price of one.

Besides, if they were waiting for him now, it just might speed things up.

The Executioner had never been averse to shortcuts, if he knew where they were taking him.

Bolan checked out the Marriott's parking lot and lobby as he entered, spotting no obvious hostiles or lookouts in the vicinity. No one tried to intercept him as he moved with purpose toward the bank of elevators, then passed by and took the stairs. He had no reason to believe that any shooters would be waiting for him on Johnny's floor, but it was a simple precaution that only cost him a couple of minutes. He took the stairs two at a time, pausing at each floor he passed to listen and make sure his footsteps caused the only echo in the stairwell.

So far, so good.

He found the door to his brother's room and knocked, standing a yard back from the peephole. Johnny opened up and stood aside to let him in. The room was perfectly generic, clean and functional. The bed was king-sized, there were desert landscapes on the walls and Johnny had a balcony roughly the size of a card table, offering a view of neon with the night pitch-black beyond.

"So, it's clean?" Bolan asked.

Johnny nodded. "Don't worry. I swept it again, right after you called."

"Okay."

"So, what's the word?" His brother sounded anxious, but it didn't show on his face.

Bolan sat in one of the room's three identical chairs. Johnny chose another, leaving a small round table between them.

"You already know about Isla de Victoria," Bolan began. "Hal couldn't add much to the basics, except for some stats. Gross national product, literacy rate, infant mortality, that kind of thing."

"Not important," Johnny said.

"The leader of the insurrectionists, as far as anyone can tell, is Maxwell Reed. He lives in Florida but travels constantly, three hundred days a year or something. The wife and kids stay home, meaning a beachfront place outside Fort Lauderdale. Hal says it looks like something from Miami Vice."

"So, liberation is a paying gig," Johnny replied.

"Looks like it. When he travels, Reed is both accompanied and met by bodyguards. According to the Bureau, some of them are syndicate, the rest are mercs."

"We're getting somewhere." Johnny smiled.

"Maybe. Most of Reed's time on the road looks like a propaganda tour, selling himself and the Victorian Liberation Movement. He has some friends who might surprise his corporate supporters, though. Particularly in Miami and New Orleans."

"Mob, again?"

"Hard-core. Vincent Ruggero runs the Family in New Orleans. Miami is covered by Joey DeMitri. Reed's gotten chummy with both of them over the past couple years."

"Let me guess about Bayou LaFourche," Johnny said. "It's Ruggero's old homestead?"

"You're close. Hal had to track ownership through a few paper fronts, but the man behind the scenes is Thomas Donato, a Ruggero underboss who specializes in narcotics with a side order of prostitution. They call him Tommy Spikes."

"Okay. So Ruggero or his number two hold the paper on Bayou LaFourche, and we know it's been used for guerrilla training in the past. What's the link to Reed's movement and Isla de Victoria?" Johnny asked.

"Hal couldn't track it any farther," Bolan said. "The Bureau's heard nothing from its informants in the area, and Ruggero won't have bothered with the state or federal paperwork on whatever he's doing. We'd need an on-site visual to check it out in any kind of detail."

"What about the Company?" Johnny's tone was apprehensive now.

"Hal ran it down the best he could and came up empty," Bolan answered. "That doesn't mean they're clean, of course, but for the moment there's nothing to suggest a Langley link."

"Meaning it's unofficial," Johnny said. "No sanction."

"As far as we know."

"So we wouldn't be stepping on anyone's toes."

Bolan frowned. "Just the Mob and the mercs."

"They don't count," Johnny told him.

"Oh, really?"

"You know what I mean. I was afraid we'd be butting heads with the CIA. This way, we're in the clear. It needs looking into. You know that."

"I know it, but that doesn't mean I have to like it." Bolan looked grim.

"Where do we start? The Big Easy? Miami?"

"The only link we have, for what it's worth," Bolan reminded him, "is one dead mercenary's mention of Bayou LaFourche. We don't know what—if anything—goes on there, or how deeply the Ruggero Family is involved. For all we know, your friend may have had some kind of mental short circuit after he was shot, thinking back to a high-school hunting trip."

"He wasn't from Louisiana. Somewhere cold and starting with an M, I think it was. Montana, Minnesota, whatever."

"Anyway, we need to have a look around on-site," Bolan replied, "before we commit ourselves."

"When you say 'we'—"

"I mean the two of us. Hal can't spare anybody else to check it out right now."

"You're cool with that?" Johnny was doubtful.

"I'd rather spend the weekend on a beach at Honolulu," Bolan answered, "but it isn't in the cards."

"Sand's overrated, anyway."

"Tell me about it."

Johnny's smile made him look five years younger. "So, when do we leave?"

"Do you have anything to wrap up at home?" Bolan asked.

"I'm clear."

"Then we're good to go. We can either book a flight for tomorrow or hit the highway after breakfast."

"I'd feel better driving," Johnny said. "That way, the gear I brought from California can go with us."

"Right." Bolan could bring his own hardware along, as well. "Suits me."

"One car or two?" Johnny asked.

"I've got a rental out of Phoenix."

"We can take the Blazer, then. Pick up another on the way, if need be."

"Right. We're on for breakfast, then?" Bolan asked.

"You can swing by here," Johnny replied. "They've got a buffet downstairs, opens at six o'clock."

Bolan changed subjects, holding Johnny's clear gaze with his own. "This is the time to let it go, if you're not sure. Once we start paddling around bayou country it'll be too late."

"No second thoughts. I'm in."

"Tomorrow morning, then," Bolan said.

"Six o'clock."

He didn't wish his younger brother pleasant dreams. Bola
had long since learned that, for a fighting man, the sweetes
dreams were often none at all.

As for the next day's excursion, Bolan hoped it wouldn'
turn into a living nightmare.

**3**

## Iberville Parish, Louisiana

The cottonmouth was close to six feet long, its drab color a fair approximation of the cypress branch it occupied and the algae-stained water below. It watched the passing skiff with lidless eyes, its spade-shaped head tracking motion while the heat-sensitive pits in its face waited for the thermal warning of warm-blooded prey. Even the reptile's tongue was gray, flicking incessantly to taste the humid air.

Welcome to bayou country, Johnny thought, and bent to his paddle. The viper was well out of reach, but it wasn't the first one he'd seen since they had entered the swamp, and he stayed alert for swimmers who might happen by and fancy a boat ride.

Initially, he'd worried more about the alligators, but so far he'd seen only two and they kept well away from the skiff. The cottonmouths, by contrast, seemed to have a certain arrogance about them, mostly staying put as the boat swept past them, sometimes showing off the snow-white lining of their mouths with lethal fangs displayed to make the point of who was more at home in this drowned land, who would prevail if it became a test of raw endurance and survival skills.

Bolan had the point, navigating via GPS and some sixth sense Johnny had yet to cultivate, guiding the skiff through channels that looked pretty much the same to Johnny,. They knew where they were going, fairly precisely, thanks to Hal Brognola and a flyover from Keesler Air Force Base outside Biloxi, Mississippi. They had aerial photos to work with, sent from Keesler to Stony Man Farm and then transmitted to Johnny's laptop at a cybercafé in El Paso. Coordinates came with the photos, and they were in business.

More or less.

The photos didn't show a conventional military compound, of course. If anything, it looked more like a backwoods hunting camp or Cajun fishing outpost. Men with guns were visible in several of the shots, none seemingly aware of the Air Force eye in the sky, but numbers were difficult to estimate, identities beyond their present reach. They wouldn't know who they were dealing with until they reached the camp and had a firsthand look, up close and personal.

By which time they would be inside the kill zone.

Even as he concentrated on their progress and the brackish water close at hand, Johnny attempted to examine every facet of the swamp. It had a certain primal beauty, underneath the smell of rotted vegetation, stagnant water and remains from the previous night's kills. The birds that rose and flapped away at their approach were often brightly colored, strangely silent in their flight except for beating wings. Where sunlight pierced the cypress canopy, it lit the waterways and hummocks like the beams of Glory featured in religious paintings.

They had considered going in at night, but finally agreed the added risks outweighed potential rewards. In darkness they were twice as likely to get lost, a hundred times more likely to encounter lurking predators. On unfamiliar ground—or water, in this case—they had a better chance of getting in and out alive during daylight. And if they absolutely needed darkness for their work, it would be easier to pass the afternoon laid up in some side channel than to find their way across the trackless swamp by night.

They had holed up overnight in Baton Rouge, after the straight-through drive from Tucson to Louisiana. Taking turns behind the wheel, they'd stopped for gas and food when there was no recourse. They had covered some nine hundred miles in eighteen hours and fell into overpriced beds at the first motel outside the Pelican State's capital. After an early breakfast that morning, the two men backtracked thirty miles to Bayou Sorrel and rented the skiff from an old man who didn't care where they were going or when they came back, as long as they tripled his normal rate in cash, up front.

Johnny guessed the old man would start drinking his windfall as soon as they pushed off from shore. He might run his gums about screwing a couple of Yankees, but what would it hurt? Unless there was a mercenary mole behind that four-day stubble, gap-toothed smile and dirty overalls, the most he'd do was play up their stupidity to other locals like himself. He didn't know where they were going, what was in their duffel bags, or where they'd parked their ride.

So let him talk.

The bags were unpacked now. They'd both changed into camouflage fatigues and combat webbing, donning commo headsets and bandoliers of spare magazines for their long guns and side arms, buckling on knives and canteens, daubing faces with greasepaint to lend them the hue of the swamp.

The Bolan brothers were dressed to kill.

Now all they needed was a target.

The Executioner seemed to read his brother's mind. As if on cue, he stowed his paddle and reached for an overhanging cypress bough—no scaled decorations on this one,

Johnny noted—and pulled their boat into the shade. Keeping his voice pitched low, Bolan said, "That's it for coasting. We're on foot the next three-quarters of a mile."

Terrific, Johnny thought, but settled for a brisk, "Okay." Lifting his CAR-15 assault rifle from the bottom of the skiff, he scrambled ashore while Bolan tied off their boat. The ground felt spongy underfoot and uttered squelching sounds from time to time. Johnny was careful, testing every step before he trusted the sodden ground with his weight.

"This way," Bolan said, and struck off through the dappled undergrowth, splashing in and out of gray-green ponds with the consistency and temperature of leftover minestrone.

Three-quarters of a mile, Johnny thought, as he followed in his brother's wake.

BOLAN SMELLED THE CAMP before he saw it. They had something on the fire, perhaps a midday meal. It smelled like some kind of chowder, strong enough from a distance to make his mouth water, but too muddled with the bayou's other scents for Bolan to guess the ingredients.

No matter.

They hadn't traveled all this way from Tucson to drop in for lunch.

Why had they come?

Because his brother's brush with death had left him with a hunch about the shooters, and it needed an explanation. There was nothing in the files at Stony Man to help them out, but Bolan didn't like the hints of Mob involvement in what had been advertised on every major network as run-of-the-mill Caribbean peasant rebellion. If there was more to it than that, as circumstances seemed to indicate, the Executioner would see what he could do to knock the plans offtrack.

They slowed on the final leg of their approach, watching

for lookouts and booby traps the same way they'd watched out for snakes and alligators all along their route of travel. Wading half the time also retarded progress, but Bolan didn't mind the slow pace. He still had no clear fix on who was waiting for them in the camp, but mercenaries were involved at some point on the food chain, and that kind of training meant soldiers well-versed in security precautions. At the moment, a Claymore mine or a frag grenade with a trip wire attached would wreak more havoc with their flesh and plans than any swampland predator they might encounter.

But the way was clear—so far, at least.

Bolan considered that, the seeming lack of posted guards or other common-sense precautions, pondering what it could mean. The men he'd come to see were either hopelessly incompetent—and Bolan wouldn't bet his life on that—or they felt confident enough in the security of their position that they didn't need any special watch on the perimeter.

It was the kind of confidence that came from knowing you had wealthy, well-placed friends. The kind of confidence that made a man feel he could get away with anything.

It was the kind of confidence that sometimes got a cocky soldier killed.

The camp rose out of mist and murk ahead of them, still some two hundred yards away. Some of the structures had been built on hummocks; others stood on platforms elevated several feet above the water's placid surface. They were connected by rough wooden piers in the fashion of riverside homes Bolan had seen in other jungles of the world. He guessed flooding would be a problem in the rainy season, and snakes the whole year 'round. From the look of it, the camp had not been built for comfort.

Johnny moved up on Bolan's left. They crouched together in the shadow of a giant mangrove, sheltered by the arching roots and razor-edged saw grass. They were close enough to bring the camp under fire with their carbines, but that wasn't part of the plan.

Not yet, anyway.

Bolan leaned forward and narrowed his eyes as two men emerged from one of the stilt houses, clomping across the elevated sidewalk to the nearest hummock, where they disappeared inside a larger building. Both men wore fatigues with pistols on their belts. The taller of them marked as a southpaw by the placement of his holster. Smoke pluming from a metal stovepipe identified the longhouse as the camp's mess hall. Bolan wished he could see through the dingy windows and take a head count, but the building held its secrets dear.

He was considering a closer vantage point, about to take it up with Johnny, when one of the men from the stilt house reappeared, carrying a metal tray. Bolan tracked him from the mess hall, back toward the heart of the camp on a large mossy hummock fifty yards or more in length and half that distance wide. Bolan could not make out his destination, but the soldier came back empty-handed moments later, wearing an expression that was stuck somewhere between a smirk and scowl.

"The CO's head waiter?" Johnny suggested.

"Could be. He doesn't seem to like the duty, whoever he's serving."

Bolan watched the soldier return to the mess hall, its door swinging shut behind him. There was no one else in sight from where they were positioned.

He glanced at Johnny and found his younger brother studying the camp. Alert.

"I want a closer look," the Executioner declared.

KEELY ROSS TESTED the shackle on her leg and knew she wasn't going anywhere without a key to fit the lock. And

since the men who'd chained her didn't want her going anywhere—at least until they took her out and dumped her in the
swamp as gator food—she wouldn't count on anybody dropping off a key to make things easier.

At least she hadn't spilled her guts.

Not yet.

Interrogation was her greatest fear. Lectures in training
were supposed to help prepare the mind for capture and potential torture, but they didn't do a thing to help the body
when the chips were down. She had been trembling more or
less nonstop since Spade's men bagged her, and she was fu-
rious with herself for displaying that weakness. It was pure
dumb luck that her captors hadn't taken advantage of that
weakness so far.

But when they did…

The first grilling had been rough, but mercifully brief. A
few slaps and pinches, some crude anatomical jokes and suggestions, rounded off with one solid right hook to the gut. Instead of following through, however, they'd chosen that
moment to put her in isolation and let her "think about it" for
a while. She understood the tactic, knew anticipation sometimes could be worse than any torment of the flesh, but the
fact was that they'd missed the chance to break her at the start.

And if she saw any opportunity to slip away, they wouldn't
get a second chance.

But how?

The shackle mocked her, and she knew the door of her
musty-smelling prison shack was padlocked. Ross didn't
think there was a guard outside the door, but with the padlock and the shackle bolted to a ring on the north wall—

Take one thing at a time, the calming voice reminded her.
What's wrong with this picture?

The wall ring.

It was mounted on a flange, which in turn was attached to the shed's plywood wall by four screws. The screws weren't large, but the swamp's pervasive damp had speckled them with rust. Ross knew a thumbnail wouldn't budge them, but Spade's lackey had brought a spoon with her meal of chowder and corn bread. If she could use one end of it to free the screws, she wouldn't need a key to remove the shackle from her leg. Just tuck the chain into her waistband or hold it in her left hand while she ran—or try to use it as a weapon when she broke out of the shed.

One thing at a time, the soothing voice said.

How long before the lackey came back for her tray? Ross knew she couldn't count on more than half an hour, and she'd already wasted part of that. Her time was running out, and there was no reason to think she'd get another meal, another chance, before the bastards went to work on her in earnest.

Trembling, on the verge of tears, she clutched the spoon and started on the screws. Five minutes passed, then she felt the first one budge, reluctantly, just as a burst of automatic fire echoed from somewhere in the camp.

THE WAY IT FELL APART was that a pair of soldiers coming out of the latrine startled Bolan. If there'd been one alone he might have salvaged it—a blitz attack to crush his larynx, shove him back inside the crapper where his death throes would be screened from passersby—but two was one too many for a silent kill.

They saw him at the same time and gaped at his uniform, gear and painted face. As young as they were, they knew death when it came for them. Bolan sized them up within a heartbeat: they were twenty-something, black and dressed in matching olive-drab fatigues. Neither one was armed, as far as he could tell, but they were both a threat to Bolan, simply standing there.

He took them out.

A short burst from the 5.56 mm carbine dropped them where they stood, a tangled sprawl of arms and legs and startled faces splashed with crimson. Bolan was already moving as they fell, trusting his brother to react like the professional he was and watch out for himself.

The worst thing, when a probe of unknown enemies on unfamiliar ground went sour, was that Bolan never knew exactly where to go or who his targets ought to be. Survival was the first priority, but gathering intelligence ran a close second— and that meant focusing on limited goals, the art of the possible. This time, the photos and his brief surveillance hadn't fingered anyone as leader of the pack or told him where to seek out the leader.

And now, the Executioner was fighting for his life.

It took a moment for the sound of the shots to register. He pictured normal life inside a training camp: some of the soldiers eating, others catching up on sleep, policing gear, cleaning their weapons, working through a list of chores that somehow never quite got finished. There would be an instant of confusion, even though they knew no firing exercises were in progress. By the time they pulled themselves together and responded, Bolan would've had a chance to stir the pot.

His brother beat him to it, though. The echoes of his carbine were still rattling around among the cypress trees when Johnny cut loose from the far side of the camp. Bolan knew it had to be his brother, since any occupant of the camp quick enough to return fire would've been shooting at him, not spraying the perimeter a hundred yards distant.

Bolan used the diversion to his best advantage, sprinting from the latrine toward a smaller structure that sprouted antennas and a satellite dish the size of a frying pan. He didn't need a look inside to recognize the camp's communications hut, and no specific orders were required for him to take it out. The last thing Bolan needed was a call for reinforcements, when he already faced a hostile force of unknown numbers.

He tried the commo hut's door, found it unlocked and unclipped a thermite grenade from his harness. Its fuel, a white phosphorous mixture, would burn anywhere: underground, underwater—even, Bolan supposed, in the vacuum of space. A chemical foam was required to douse the white-hot flames, and the soldier guessed there was none of the good stuff in camp at the moment.

He pulled the pin and tossed the grenade into the hut, slamming the door behind it as voices began to call out from various parts of the camp. He ran for cover, toward the south end of a building that resembled a crude bunkhouse, just as men in heat-wilted uniforms began spilling out of the mess hall. Bolan had time to register that most of them were black, then the thermite grenade whumped to life and the commo hut was devoured by a blinding ball of fire.

The earpiece of his radio headset was silent, but he could still hear Johnny's CAR-15. The kid was busy, with no time to chat at the moment. Bolan took a cue from his sibling and popped out of cover long enough to rake the milling crowd of men outside the mess hall, dropping several as his armor-piercing rounds cut through fabric, flesh and bone. The rest scattered, some ducking back inside the building, while the others ran for their lives.

Somewhere across the camp, from Johnny's direction, a different weapon rattled in answer to the incoming fire. This one sounded like a submachine gun, probably 9 mm, and a shotgun kicked in right behind it, pumping out three blasts in rapid-fire.

The best Bolan could do for his brother at a distance was

to raise hell and distract the shooters, let them know they had more than one target to deal with in camp. Accordingly, he palmed a frag grenade and yanked the pin, stepped out and pitched the bomb toward a group of trainees huddled near a second barracks, twenty yards away.

A couple of them saw it coming, calling out a warning to their mates and breaking for the nearest cover. The rest tried to scatter and some of them made it, but others were flattened by shrapnel and shock waves, lying crumpled on the grassy hummock when the smoke cleared. Bolan tracked a pair of staggering survivors with his carbine, giving each of them a 3-round burst from fifty feet to put them down.

A static whisper in the Executioner's left ear resolved itself as Johnny's voice. "There's something…not sure… maybe…prisoner."

"You're breaking up here," Bolan told him. "Say again."

"No time…moving…I'll check it out."

Dammit!

He didn't have a clear fix on the kid's location, but the camp was small enough that dead reckoning should do the trick. Bolan clung to the shade of another longhouse, moving swiftly along toward the spot where his brother's last burst of rifle fire had sounded. As he ran, Bolan replayed the garbled message in his head.

A prisoner?

He couldn't guess who might be caged out here in the middle of nowhere. It could be anyone from a wayward trainee to a target from the Ruggero Family's hit list. A part of Bolan wished Johnny would let it go, but he knew that ran against the grain for both of them.

Besides, a captive rescued might become a source of information to define the game, its stakes and help identify the opposition's players.

But they'd have to bring out the hostage alive, and that thought made the kid's last words repeat incessantly in Bolan's mind.

No time, no time, no time.

JOHNNY WAS UNDER FIRE when he glimpsed the two soldiers from earlier, moments after the brothers sighted the camp. They were running together, away from the fight, one now armed with an automatic rifle, while his sidekick—the lefty—had his pistol drawn. Johnny couldn't tell where they were going, but it struck him that they were not fleeing, so much as pursuing some urgent errand.

Intrigued by that notion, he wanted to follow, but that meant disposing of two shooters who'd zeroed in on him seconds earlier. They were crouched behind a large tank that he took for some kind of water filtration device. They popped out by turns to fire at Johnny's position with a submachine gun and a pump-action shotgun. They'd torn hell out of the hummock where Johnny had gone to ground, but he'd moved without them noticing, closing the gap when their natural expectation would've been for him to cut and run.

He judged the new distance between himself and the targets as he unclipped a frag grenade from his belt and thumbed the pin free. Johnny waited for the shotgunner to take his next shot, now some fifteen yards offtarget, then he pitched the grenade overhand, watching it drop two feet short of the target and wobble forward.

The shooter with the SMG popped out of cover, lining up a burst, but the grenade's fuse burned down before he could fire. The blast took his face off, and most of one arm, its concussion crumpling one of the struts that supported the big water tank. Johnny saw it start to tilt, groaning, clear water spouting from a score of holes jagged shrapnel had punched in the tank.

The shotgunner tried to scramble clear before it toppled, but he seemed to be stunned by the blast, shaky and stumbling in retreat. Johnny hit him with a burst that spun him on his heels and dumped him facedown in the grass, unmoving.

Done.

Watching for other shooters as he rose, Johnny heard new explosions from the far side of the camp. Unseen for the moment, he followed the soldiers he'd glimpsed moments earlier, projecting their route of travel now that they were out of view. He found them again as one bent to key open a padlock on the door of a shed set apart from the rest of the camp. The man with the key—the southpaw—slipped inside, while his friend with the rifle stood watch.

Johnny keyed his microphone, hoping his wade through the swamp and the action afterward hadn't harmed the connection. "There's something going on here," he told Bolan. "I'm not sure what's up. Maybe they've got a prisoner."

It took a beat for his brother's voice to come back at him. "You're breaking up here. Say again."

Before he could answer, a red-haired woman stumbled into view, emerging from the shed. The rifleman grabbed one of her arms before she could bolt. From behind her, the guy with the pistol emerged and grabbed the other arm. Between them, they started marching her back toward Johnny.

"No time," he told his brother, hoping his words were audible. "They're moving now. I'll check it out."

The soldiers and their captive had closed half the gap between themselves and Johnny when the man in charge changed his mind. With a sharp yank on the redhead's left arm, he changed course in midstride, drawing her and his companion off to the west.

Johnny gave them a lead, lining up his shot. The rifleman

posed a greater threat, to both the woman and himself. Accordingly, Johnny fixed his sights between the target's shoulder blades and stroked his carbine's trigger, shifting to his left before he registered the killing impact.

Johnny heard the woman gasp and saw her sole surviving escort pivot toward the sound of gunfire. The smart move was to loop an arm around her neck and use the redhead as a shield, but Johnny beat him to it, triggering another burst that stitched a ragged line of holes across the soldier's chest and punched him over backward, off his feet.

The woman stood petrified as he approached her, wide eyes taking in the vision of her rescuer. From her expression, it was clear she didn't know if she should bolt or stand her ground, but fear overrode conscious thought, rooting her to the soil.

"If you can walk, we need to go," he told her.

"Right. I guess you saved my life."

"Not yet," he answered, "but I'm working on it."

Johnny spun to the sound of footsteps behind him, then instantly relaxed.

"We should go," the Executioner stated.

WAYLAND SPADE KNEW better than to panic. Experience had taught him that almost any situation could be salvaged with the proper application of ingenuity and brute force, and in the remainder of cases it was sufficient to get out alive.

Still living, though some of his soldiers and trainees were not, Spade turned his thoughts to the detail of a hasty salvage operation. Before he could begin to cut his losses, though, he had to find out what they were.

One of his troops, a Texas boy named Ritter appeared beside him, snapping to a half-assed version of attention. "Skip it," Spade told him. "What's the word?"

"She's gone, sir. I found Polk and Esterhouse, both dead."

Spade bit his tongue to keep from cursing. It was what he'd feared the most: the absolute worst-case scenario. Not swamp rats, poachers, or a federal raiding party on a fishing expedition, but a probe to lift the woman out beneath his very nose. Worse yet, he'd failed to crack her in the time available, meaning he didn't know how much she knew, how much she could reveal.

And that was unforgivable.

Spade didn't want to think about explaining the snafu to his superior. He'd probably survive the storm that would inevitably follow his announcement of the woman's liberation, but it could only damage the respect and reputation he had worked so hard to build the past five years.

Unless he got the woman back, along with those who'd lifted her.

Dead-or-alive was unimportant now. His first priority was the recovery of stolen merchandise, his second making sure that nothing in the woman's head was shared with adversaries in the outside world. The surest guarantee of that would be to take the head right off her shoulders, clip her vocal cords and shut her mouth for good.

As for the men who'd lifted her...

Spade would've paid dearly to question them, as well, but realistically he knew that wasn't in the cards. They'd killed a number of his troops already. There was no reason to believe they'd suddenly throw down their arms if cornered. They'd been able to locate and penetrate the camp, which meant he'd have to uproot the facility and find another training site. Maybe that would solve the problem.

Maybe not.

"How many of them were there?" he asked Ritter. "Do we know that?"

"No, sir. Definitely two, sir, but beyond that it's confused."

"We need to track them while there's time," Spade said. "Find out which way they went."

"Sir, how—?"

"We've got a camp full of observers. Someone saw them leaving with the woman. If you can't find living witnesses, extrapolate their flight path from the bodies left behind. They had no time to fake a trail. Now move!"

"Yes, sir!"

The waiting was a bitch. Spade took pride in his patience under normal circumstances—and in others not so normal— but the nerves were kicking in this time. He had begun to second-guess his own decisions, wishing that he'd killed the woman outright, rather than attempting to extract whatever information she possessed. The raiders might've still come looking for her, granted, but at least they couldn't have retrieved her. Not in any shape to spill her guts.

*I should've spilled them for her.*

Spade didn't like the agitation he was feeling. It upset his sense of order and control. It would require an extra effort not to let his soldiers know that he was seething inwardly, that close to screaming in his rage or picking up a weapon and using it on the first clumsy fuck-up who crossed his path tonight.

*Tonight?*

He realized that dusk was falling rapidly across Bayou La Fourche. Less than an hour of daylight remained, and that would be murky at best. If they were going to overtake the raiders, they needed to start right away.

Ritter returned five agonizing minutes later, followed by one of the trainees. Spade wouldn't call him a soldier, they hadn't progressed that far in training yet, but at least the guy was holding himself together fairly well.

"Well?" Spade snapped at Ritter.

"Southwest, sir." Ritter jerked a thumb toward the trainee. "He saw two soldiers with a woman, heading off into the swamp, and we've got half a dozen dead on the perimeter back there."

Spade faced the trainee. "What's your name?"

"Sir, Milton, sir!"

"How certain are you that you saw a woman, Milton?"

"Sir, I'm absolutely certain, sir!"

"And two men with her?"

"Sir, yes, sir!"

Too damned much drilling on the military courtesy, Spade thought.

"Not my men?"

"Sir, no, sir!"

"Airboats!" he snapped at Ritter. "Leave one, just in case, and take the rest. No one comes back without the woman and the other two. Is that precisely understood?"

"Yes, sir!"

And if no one returned, there'd still be one airboat for Spade. His standby option.

Just in case.

## 4

Getting out of the camp had been relatively easy. Staying out, Bolan thought, might prove more of a challenge. They'd been slogging through the swamp for nearly ten minutes, bearing southwest in the lowering dusk, when he heard the growl of engines approaching from behind.

"That sounds like speedboats," Johnny said, trailing behind the woman so she wouldn't fall behind or wander off by accident or otherwise.

"Airboats," she corrected him, sounding a little short of air herself. Bolan guessed she was winded from scrambling over hummocks, ducking cypress limbs and wading through water that came to her chest when it rose only waist-deep for Bolan and Johnny. "They're faster and don't draw much water."

"How far to the skiff?" Johnny asked.

Bolan checked the GPS scanner without breaking stride. "Two hundred yards, give or take."

"We'd better hurry, then."

They hurried, but the droning engine sounds drew steadily closer, as if a swarm of giant wasps were hurtling after them. Bolan wasn't sure they could reach the skiff, much less that the boat's outboard motor would be any match for airboats built to navigate the swamp at top speed.

Would he even be able to find the way out after dark, without lights to betray them and help the trackers zero in on their target? If and when they were overtaken, how many adversaries would they face? Would they be seasoned troops or green trainees? Would there be any chance to—?

Stop it!

Bolan focused on putting one foot in front of the other, making slow but steady progress while the drone of engines grew louder and louder behind him. He glanced back periodically, to check on Johnny and the woman, gratified to find them keeping pace. Whatever else went wrong, he wouldn't have to waste time chasing after them, bringing them back on course.

A serpentine body brushed Bolan's left thigh, recoiled from the contact, then vanished. He braced himself for the lancing pain of a snakebite, but nothing happened. He forged ahead, the next grassy hummock rising before him like an oasis in a drowned desert. He lunged ashore and waited for the others, using the time to scan their track and check for signs of the approaching enemy.

They weren't hard to find. Spotlights blazed through the near-night of dusk in the swamp, beams slashing through the murk and bouncing when the high-speed boats skipped over floating limbs, swimming wildlife, whatever lay in their path. Bolan counted eight and reckoned three or four men to a boat. They were closing in too quickly. In a heartbeat, he knew they wouldn't make it to the skiff before the hunters overtook them.

The soldier considered his team's options, such as they were. They could push on, virtually certain of being overhauled before they reached the skiff, forced to fight wherever they were at the moment. Or they could choose their ground right now and make a stand.

"We can't outrun them," Bolan said.

"You got that right," the woman echoed.

"If we have to fight," he continued, "it's better to choose our own place while we can."

"They'll run circles around us in airboats," the woman predicted. "We don't have a chance."

"Would you rather surrender?" Johnny asked.

"Hell, no. They're beyond taking prisoners now, if you ask me."

"I didn't."

"Terrific. You want to get over yourself?"

"We need to focus," Bolan interrupted. "If we can't do that, we're dead."

"Sorry," Johnny said.

"Right," the woman groused. "Me, too."

"I don't believe we'll find a better place than this, all things considered," Bolan said. The hummock had a natural depression near its center. Mangroves sprouting here and there around it would prevent an airboat sailing straight across the widest portion, taking off their heads.

"It isn't much," Johnny suggested, "but it beats the open water."

"I'll feel better," the woman said, "if you let me have one of those pistols."

Bolan saw his frown reflected back at him from Johnny's face. "Are you familiar with firearms?" he asked.

"I shot ninety-nine out of a hundred on my last trip through Hogan's Alley," she told him, naming the famous firing range at the FBI Academy in Quantico, Virginia. "Of course, I was using a Glock, not one of those Beretta 93-Rs you're packing in that Galco shoulder rig. I think I can hold my own, though."

Bolan glanced past her to Johnny, receiving a shrug in

reply to his unspoken question. They didn't know who the woman was or who signed her paychecks, and while the reference to Quantico was heartening, it could be a lie. Whatever her background or loyalties, though, he surmised that she wasn't anxious for a return engagement in the mercenary camp.

He gave her the Beretta, watching as she checked it over, found the live round in the chamber and flashed him a smile.

"This will do," she said.

"I hope so," Bolan replied, "because we've got about two minutes left before it all hits the fan."

THE PISTOL WAS LARGER than anything Keely Ross normally carried, heavier by several ounces, but it still felt good in her hands. She set the fire-selector switch for single shot, afraid of wasting precious ammunition on 3-round bursts while she got the feel of the gun in combat.

There'd be no second chances this night, no range master to supply extra rounds if she squandered the ammo she had. Instead she would be dead in the swamp, food for whatever scavengers happened along afterward.

But if she had any chance at all to make it through the night alive, why not give it a shot?

Ross tightened her grip on the borrowed Beretta. Why not give it twenty?

The airboats were almost on top of them, fanning out to flank the hummock on either side, and for a moment she wondered if her rescuers might let the hunting party roar past them, off into the swamp. It could buy them some time, she supposed, but how much? How long would it be before the searchers realized they must've missed their quarry and doubled back to scour the bayou by sectors?

Not long.

If they were caught on open water, in the skiff her companions had mentioned, Ross knew they'd be as good as dead. The hunters could circle and cut them to pieces with automatic weapons. At least where they were, they had a fighting chance.

And she could take some of the bastards with her when she went.

Any thought of letting the search team escape was erased from her mind as Bolan fired a burst, taking out the nearest airboat's spotlight. Someone cried out in pain or surprise as the craft swept past them, engine roaring, but Ross couldn't track it very far before she was distracted by the rest.

That first short burst of fire changed everything. The airboats that had passed their hiding place had already doubled back, raising spray as they whipped through broad U-turns. Those still on the approach either slowed down or veered away, their pilots deciding while shooters on the flat decks opened fire, raking the hummock.

Wincing at each nearby hit, Ross cursed her arrogance and thought, Hogan's Alley was never like this.

The targets in practice never shot back.

After what seemed like hours but had to have been seconds, she raised her head and risked a shot with the Beretta. Ross was more surprised than anyone when her bullet struck one of the airboats, clanging loudly on a blade of its giant propeller. The shot caused no damage. It didn't even slow the hostile craft as it raced past the hummock on her left with guns blazing from the deck, but at least it made Ross feel that she was in the fight, contributing.

Naturally, her second shot was a complete miss, high and wide.

After that, there was no time to focus on style. The targets came too rapidly from every side; the hostile fire was too intense. Ross surrendered herself to instinct, the way she'd been taught to fight when her life was on the line. But even in the midst of total chaos she recognized the ironic fact that her first firefight would also likely be her last.

Ross tried a double tap next time, four rounds gone out of twenty, and she felt like cheering when a rifleman pitched from the deck of a passing airboat, arms flailing, lips forming a startled O as he hit the slate-gray water. Ross kept watching, flinching when the bullets passed too close, waiting for him to surface, but he never did.

One down, she thought. My first.

She might have some reaction later, toss her cookies or whatever, but her only sensation at that moment was relief, riding a low swell of elation. There was one less enemy to threaten her, and shooting him meant no more to her than if she had just stepped on cockroach.

Don't get cocky, the voice in her head chided. You're a long way from being home and dry.

As if to reinforce that point, a bullet struck the muddy turf in front of her and stung her face with grit. Recoiling, she swiped at her eyes, momentarily blinded while the battle raged around her.

Not fair! her mind rebelled, but what in life was ever truly fair?

Tears helped to clear the grainy muck out of her eyes, and Ross was startled to discover that they were not tears of pain or panic.

They were tears of killing rage.

As soon as she could see again, she leveled the Beretta and rejoined the fight.

JOHNNY CAUGHT THE AIRBOAT in midturn, swept by the spotlight beam of another behind it, and shot the pilot through the chest. Belted into his seat as he was, the dead man slumped forward like a rag doll, hands slipping from the airboat's controls, throttle and rudder suddenly unmanned.

The boat stalled, engine sounds throttling back as one of the shooters moved toward the dead pilot. Johnny shot him on the move and pitched him over the side, out of view. Two others were raking the hummock with M-16 rifles, raising spouts of mud and water, chewing bark from the mangroves that flanked Johnny's roost.

It was nearly full dark in the swamp now, but muzzle-flashes and sweeping spotlights supplemented the light of a pale quarter moon, helping Johnny spot his targets. The mobile shooters were handicapped now, as the crazy light show worked against them and erratic motion spoiled their aim.

Johnny hoped it was enough to keep his team—Mack's team—alive.

The gunmen on the stalled airboat were edging toward the pilot's chair, milking short bursts from their rifles as they crossed the airboat's broad, flat deck. Johnny stitched the one nearest the controls with a burst that cut his legs from under him and left him flopping like a stranded catfish. His companion straightened, shouldering his M-16 for an aimed shot at Johnny's muzzle-flash, but the younger Bolan was too quick for him, a second burst gutting the man where he stood and tossing him over the side.

More gator bait, he thought, then forced the image out of mind.

The stationary airboat's sole survivor struggled up to one knee, fumbling with the dead pilot's seat belt. He'd seemingly forgotten his weapon, focused now on revving up the boat and getting out of range before he took another hit.

Too late.

Johnny strafed him with another burst from twenty yards

or less and dropped his target to the deck again. There was no thrashing this time, just a shiver that passed through the gunner's body, there and gone within a heartbeat, leaving him collapsed and still.

A second airboat slowed beside the first, its crew taking stock of the dead, then it roared off as Johnny was framing his shot. He tried a short burst anyway, his bullets striking sparks from the cage surrounding the airboat's propeller.

Wasted.

So far, one of the airboats was dead in the water and two or three others were missing crewmen, but the surviving gunners were still pouring fire into the hummock at will. Johnny knew it was only a matter of time until some of those wild rounds struck home…unless they started paring down the odds.

He clutched a frag grenade, his second last, and worked its pin free with the thumb of his opposing hand. Timing was everything in this case, with a six-second fuse providing the deadline and the whole damned battlefield a giant water hazard. He would have to score an airburst if he wanted it to count, and even then he'd need a target within range, or the attempt would be an exercise in sheer futility.

Whatever.

Nothing ventured, nothing gained.

He chose a moment when two airboats roared into view from opposite directions, moving to pass each other on the west side of the hummock. The gunners would have to cease fire for an instant, to spare each other, and Johnny started counting down the seconds in his head.

On three he released the grenade's safety spoon, retaining the lethal egg in his grasp for another two seconds, then wafting it high overhead, invisible against the velvet sky as it arched above the wobbling spotlight beams. He prayed the fuse would be precise and that his aim was true.

A fireball suddenly erupted, six or seven feet above the water, as the airboats were about to pass in opposite directions, thirty feet offshore. Shrapnel swept lacerated bodies from the decks of both, flaying the pilots where they sat, strapped to their seats. One of the boats veered left and tried to mount the other, its flat hull grinding over the blood-slick deck, giant fans howling in protest.

Johnny took advantage of the moment, shouldering his carbine and pouring automatic fire into the place where he thought the stranded airboat's fuel tank should be. On his second burst he was rewarded with another spout of flame, this one spreading like lava as gasoline spilled and caught fire, burning wherever it found room to breathe. In seconds the swamp was on fire, the crippled airboats settling awkwardly in water too shallow to smother their burning remains.

Better, Johnny thought, but they still weren't out of danger. In fact, from the volume of fire pouring into the hummock, it seemed that the surviving hunters were more determined than ever to score a clean sweep.

BOLAN SCANNED the battlefield with narrowed eyes, trying to preserve his night vision against leaping flames and sweeping spotlight beams. It was easy to track the airboats, but more difficult to sweep the gunmen from their decks as they veered in and out of range, using spotlights and gunfire in tandem to pin down their targets.

None of Bolan's team had suffered injury so far, and that was something, though he realized it couldn't last much longer. Any second now, a well-aimed shot or lucky stray might find its mark, maybe killing one of them outright, at the very least reducing their defensive strength.

And then…

The good news was their female companion seemed to

know her way around a handgun, squeezing off measured shots at the fast-moving targets, scoring one hit so far that Bolan had confirmed.

It was better than average, better than Bolan had any right to expect. But who in hell was she?

No time for that now.

One of the airboats made a straight run toward the hummock, revving its motor, bow lifting slightly as if it planned to do the impossible and pass overland, flattening everyone and everything in its path. The tactic might've been intimidating to another adversary, but Bolan had already sized up the hummock and knew the looming mangroves would not let a boat pass. With that point settled in his mind, he focused on his rifle sights and started playing short bursts back and forth across the charging airboat's deck.

The gunmen aboard did their best to return fire, but it was a losing proposition. The airboat's progress, slapping over waves, bow tilting upward, made them fight to keep their balance while they tried to save themselves. It was a bad combination, and they didn't have the skill to save the play. Bolan took his time and picked them off, one at a time.

He dropped the starboard shooter first, a tall man armed with some kind of AK-47 knockoff boasting a 100-round drum. It didn't matter how much ammo he carried, though, if he couldn't land the rounds on-target, and this time the airboat's yawing defeated him. Bolan made it official with a burst to the chest that sent his target sprawling, thrashing over the side.

That left three, only two of them ready to fight. Bolan's next burst stitched the port gunner and dropped him to his knees. Dumbfounded at his own undoing, the wounded man tried to raise his weapon for a parting shot, but his strength ran out through the holes in his body and he collapsed facedown on the deck.

On a whim, Bolan went for the pilot next, killing him where he sat before the frightened man could veer off course and make a run for open water. His drag on the rudder came close, even so, but the airboat was too close for dead hands to save it by then. It struck the hummock's mossy bank at a thirty-degree angle and climbed six feet before colliding with the arched roots of a sturdy mangrove tree.

Bolan saw a human figure somersault from the twisted wreckage as it settled half in the water and the rest ashore. The big propeller churned water for a moment before it was still. Bolan didn't know where the stray shooter had landed, and he had no time to track the missing man as four other airboats circled the hummock, their guns spitting death.

He tracked the nearest of them, Bolan's carbine spitting half a dozen rounds before the slide locked open and he had to ditch the empty magazine, slapping another into the receiver instinctively, without ever taking his eyes off the target.

They were past him by then, and another boat was veering in toward shore, guns blazing. Bolan ducked beneath a hail of bullets, then popped up to return fire when the shooters lingered a moment too long. One of them flopped on his back, arms outflung, boot heels drumming the deck, as the airboat sped off to the east.

Every hit was a bonus at this point. They needed a clean sweep, to stall reinforcements from finding their trail if they managed to slip through alive. Otherwise, they'd be back to square one, overhauled in the skiff that was too slow, too small and too open to let them survive an attack on the water.

It was here or nowhere, now or never.

And the Executioner still couldn't guarantee which way the cosmic dice would fall.

KEELY ROSS WAS DOWN to four or five shots in the Beretta's extended magazine. She'd lost count around number thirteen, when two of the airboats collided and burst into flames, then again when a third jumped the shore and crashed into a tree. In any case, she knew the pistol wasn't empty yet, because its slide was closed, proof positive that there was still a live round in the chamber. After that…

Ross was wondering how difficult it would be to ask for a fresh magazine, when the older of her two rescuers reached around and dropped one in her lap. She had no time to ask if he was clairvoyant or simply so skilled that he could anticipate her needs, but it worked out either way.

At just that moment, coming up along the east side of the hummock was another of the four remaining airboats, three men visible on board. One of them had a shotgun, while the second clutched a submachine gun and the pilot concentrated on his stick controls. More confident, now that she could reload, Ross sighted down the 93-R's slide and gave the shotgunner a double tap that staggered him before his legs folded, and he dropped to the deck.

Still nothing in the guilt department, she discovered.

Maybe later.

Ross found her second target as the submachine gun's muzzle started winking flame. The darkness favored Ross until the airboat's pilot swung his spotlight toward shore, but she'd already found her mark by then and triggered two more rounds to put the second shooter on his back.

The pilot realized his error and gunned the throttle, cranking the rudder hard to his left as he swung away from shore toward open water, but Ross had him marked. Squeezing off the last round from her first magazine, she saw the pilot lurch on his seat while she ditched the empty mag and swiftly replaced it, thumbing down the slide release to chamber a fresh round.

The boat was drawing out of pistol range by then, and Ross was disinclined to waste a bullet when it would've meant a trick shot through the blur of huge propeller blades to find her target. She was cursing the lost opportunity when the airboat veered off course and clipped a free-standing cypress that rose from the swamp in its path. That impact spun the airboat in the water and its engine stalled, the pilot slumped in his safety harness and made no effort to restart it.

Lucky break, Ross told herself, but she would take what she could get.

She was looking for another target, keeping her head down, when a scuffling sound from her right distracted her. She turned, tracking with her pistol, just in time to see a shambling figure lurch into view from the shadows.

It had to be an enemy, since her only two friends in the swamp were behind her, both firing off into the dark. But the shambler's movements seemed more confused than aggressive. He carried no visible weapon, his hands raised to claw at the dark, blurred mask of his face. A sweeping floodlight beam gave Ross a glimpse of that countenance, gore and mud mixed together in a dripping poultice where the shooter had plunged headfirst into muck when he was pitched from his airboat. He should have stayed down, out of sight, but some instinct propelled him toward the sounds of battle, as if he could still hold his own in the fray.

Ross lifted the Beretta, sighting on his chest. It was a no-risk shot from twenty feet, an easy kill. And then she hesitated, not from sympathy or weakness, but because she saw an opportunity to score where she had failed so far. A living prisoner might be induced to talk, and if he seemed to pose a threat while they were fighting for their lives, a single trigger-pull would finish it.

Ross dropped her aim and waited, letting the figure take a few more steps until she knew she couldn't miss her target. Squeezing off from barely ten feet distant, she took out his left knee in a spray of crimson, grimacing in sympathetic pain as he went down.

The wounded soldier howled, clutching his shattered knee. Ross leaned out from her makeshift foxhole, finger clear of the Beretta's trigger guard as she slammed the pistol down on her adversary's skull. It took another swing to silence him, and while she didn't know how long he would remain unconscious, Ross was confident he wasn't going anywhere.

*Just watch him,* the voice in her head chided Ross. *He doesn't need a kneecap to wring your neck with those hands.*

"So, I'll watch it," she muttered, and turned back to find a new mark on the water, tracking targets over pistol sights.

THREE AIRBOATS REMAINED, but none of them appeared to have full crews. Bolan watched one sweep past, a single gunman kneeling on the deck, and shot the pilot as a hedge against letting the craft escape. It didn't stall immediately, but he put a burst into the shrouded motor and that did the trick.

By the time he swung back toward the shooter, Bolan's target had chosen survival over valor, launching himself into a dive from the starboard side. That put the boat between them and prevented Bolan from sniping him in the water, a smart move on the gunner's part—but not quite smart enough.

He'd forgotten the swamp's other killers. Twin streams of ripples converged on the swimmer as he thrashed his way through dark water toward the closest hummock. The man was barely ten yards from the drifting airboat when a piglike grunting noise erupted from the darkness, punctuated by a high-pitched scream and desperate thrashing in the water. Bolan couldn't see the reptiles feed from where he lay, but he was satisfied the soldier wouldn't be relaying their coordinates to his superiors.

Two airboats to go.

His brother had engaged the crew of one, dueling across the water with his CAR-15 against their automatic weapons. Bolan was about to join him, when the second boat loomed out of murk and mist to demand his attention, running in close to the hummock with weapons ablaze.

It was nerve over brains all the way, and Bolan took advantage of his shelter, hearing the fierce hornet buzz of incoming rounds as they passed a foot or more above his head. He sighted on the muzzle-flashes, leading them enough to score with his first short burst on the forward shooter, gutting him where he crouched at the airboat's prow.

The pilot couldn't stop in time to save his second crewman, and Bolan didn't even have to lift his sights. He just waited for the airboat to glide six feet farther on before he stroked the carbine's trigger again. The shooter was firing by that time, his rounds coming closer than before, gouging bark from the trunk of a mangrove to Bolan's immediate left. He flinched involuntarily, but not before a 3-round burst was on its way, clipping the shooter and dropping him to one knee on the airboat's deck.

He was down but not out, cursing audibly as he fought his M-16 back onto target for another try. Bolan ducked another burst of incoming fire, blinking muck from his eyes as the gunner walked a burst across the low facade of his shelter. One of the slugs came close to parting his hair as Bolan fell back, wiping his face with one hand while he clung to the carbine.

Before he could return fire the woman was beside him, clutching the Beretta in both hands and firing toward the airboat from thirty-odd feet. It was bold and it worked, the gunner rocked backward as her rounds hit home with stunning force. He toppled over slowly, still fighting the pull of gravity with his last ounce of strength, but the last rounds from his rifle were fired skyward, wasted on the night.

Bolan caught the airboat's pilot as he tried to save himself. Too late. A heartbeat later the dead man hung limp in his safety harness, fingers frozen on the throttle as his vehicle raced away northward, lost moments later in the vastness of the swamp.

Silence fell across the bayou country as the engine sounds faded with distance. Bolan didn't trust the void of sound at first, but then he saw his brother rise, no rounds incoming to strike him down where he stood.

It was over.

Almost.

A moaning sound from his left brought Bolan around, carbine leveled to cover a figure sprawled on the ground, stirring fitfully as he struggled back to a semblance of consciousness. The guy had blood on his scalp and face, more showing at the knee where a bullet had ripped through flesh and bone. He wasn't armed or fit for combat, but Bolan kept him covered anyway.

"Who's this?" Johnny asked, moving up to join them.

"I'd say someone from the wreck," Bolan replied.

"A prisoner," the woman said. "He ought to be worth something, don't you think?"

"If we can get him back," Johnny said. "If he talks."

"We've got room in the skiff," Bolan observed. "As far as conversation, we can wing it later."

"Wait a second, now." There was a cautionary tone in the woman's voice. She still held Bolan's pistol in her right hand, pointed at the soggy ground. "When I said 'prisoner,' I meant my prisoner."

Johnny half turned, so that the muzzle of his carbine hovered at a point somewhere between the woman and the night. "And who are you, exactly?" he inquired.

"There wasn't time for introductions," she replied. "I'm Keely Ross, with the U.S. Office of Homeland Security. And you are—?"

**5**

The ride back through the swamp was tense and silent. They were crowded in the skiff, four bodies where they'd started out with two. Johnny and his brother had agreed to use the oars again, instead of cranking up the outboard motor. There was no sign yet of a pursuit, but why take chances, when the price of being overtaken by their enemies on open water would be sudden death?

The woman who'd identified herself as Keely Ross had no credentials to support her claim of federal law-enforcement ties, but she had promised proof upon their return to civilization. Their prisoner, meanwhile, had offered nothing but a blue streak of profanity in transit to the skiff, and Bolan had done them all a favor when he gave the guy a tap and put him out.

The swamp was back to normal as they paddled through the darkness, frogs and insects keeping up their steady harmony, while bats and night birds swooped overhead, adding shrill voices to the harmony. Alligators splashed and bellowed in the darkness, seeking mates or prey.

Johnny wished they could unload their prisoner and let him sink or swim among those prehistoric hunters, but his rational mind knew better. They'd gone into Bayou LaFourche for a simple look around, with no clear idea of what they'd find, and they were coming out with two potential sources of vital intelligence.

Two helpings of trouble, he thought, digging in with the paddle. Two more wild cards in a deck that was already stacked against them.

But maybe a wild card or two would be just what they needed to salvage the game.

He studied Keely Ross—the back of her head, anyway—and wondered if that really was her name. Why should it be? Johnny and Mack had both given her pseudonyms back on the hummock. In fact, he was less concerned with what she called herself than he was with her claim to represent the Office of Homeland Security.

Johnny assumed that the OHS collected its intelligence "through channels"—from the FBI, the CIA, the NSA and other federal alphabet agencies. It hadn't crossed his mind that the organization maintained its own team of field agents.

Or did they?

He had nothing to prove it, so far, but the word of a woman he'd never seen before this night, who could easily be lying through her teeth. There were no promises, no guarantees.

And yet, strangely, he'd found himself hoping that she'd told the truth. After all the blood he'd spilled this night, he didn't want the woman's on his hands.

But if it came to that...

The mercenary stirred. He was slumped in a space between Johnny and the woman, with Bolan in the bow of the skiff. Johnny had a view of everyone, and he could act if either of their unexpected passengers got up to any mischief as they paddled through the night.

"What's this shit? Where am I?" the mercenary suddenly demanded.

"Shut up," Johnny warned him.

"Hey, fuck you! I—"

Johnny swung his paddle up and over on the forward stroke, barely missing a beat as he cracked the hostage hard behind one ear and put him back to sleep. He'd pulled the punch to keep from using lethal force, but there was a vicious migraine waiting in the man's future.

If he lived that long.

Bolan used the GPS device to guide them back to Bayou Sorrel. It was almost midnight as they approached the settlement's lighted docks. They pulled into shore a hundred yards short of the main pier, tying up to a smaller dock with warped boards and barnacled pilings.

They hadn't stopped to change clothes on the return trip, but their carbines and web gear were stowed in duffel bags again. Bolan and Johnny were armed with only the pistols hidden beneath their loose camouflage shirts. Keely Ross had returned Bolan's Beretta without argument and she was now unarmed, as far as Johnny knew. None of their clothing would pass close inspection without arousing suspicion, but Johnny hoped they could reach the Blazer without meeting a curious cop on patrol.

Bolan was first out of the boat, after he lashed it to a metal cleat and double-checked the knot. Keely Ross followed after, while Johnny lingered in the skiff and helped them manhandle the moaning bulk of their captive onto the pier. Watching for passersby, they carried the prisoner to Johnny's waiting vehicle, where they bound him tightly with nylon cord, stuffed a gag in his mouth and left him on a plastic tarp, on the rear deck, concealed by a blanket.

When that was done, Johnny slid into the driver's seat and

the woman took the seat beside him. Bolan took the back seat, to cover their hostile passenger and silence the wounded man if he tried to raise hell. Now all they needed was a place to go, where they could have some privacy.

"Where to?" Johnny asked of no one in particular.

"I have a quiet place," the woman said. "It's roughly half an hour from here."

Johnny eyed his brother's reflection in the rearview mirror. Bolan shrugged, and Johnny heard the zipper on one of the duffel bags purr as it opened.

"We may as well try it," Bolan said.

"If it's a trap, you're toast," Johnny warned the lady.

"Never fear," she said, smiling. "You drive, I'll navigate."

IT WAS A RISKY GAME, but Ross believed she was a fair judge of character. If her new companions, introduced as Johnny Grant and Matt Cooper, had been dangerous—to her, at least—Ross thought she would've sensed it at their meeting. And why would they have saved her life at all, only to kill her later?

Still...

When they were rolling and she'd given Johnny Grant his first set of directions, Ross decided it was time to break the ice. "It's not that I'm ungrateful," she began, "but I can't help wondering what brought you out to Bayou LaFourche, tonight of all nights."

She caught Grant's glance at the rearview mirror before he answered. "The timing was coincidence," he said.

"Good luck for me, at least," Ross acknowledged. "Who sent you?"

"That's classified," Bolan answered from the rear.

"I showed you mine," she said, with just the proper pouting tone.

"Not yet, you haven't," the older man corrected her. "Talk's cheap."

"You want credentials, I've got them stashed where we're going. In the meantime—"

"In the meantime," Johnny interrupted, "why don't you tell us what you were doing in the middle of bayou country with a pack of mercs?"

"Getting tortured and killed," she said bluntly. "If you two hadn't shown up when you did."

"Glad to help," Johnny allowed, "but that isn't an answer."

"I guess you mean why were they looking to waste me?"

"That's it."

"I have a hunch," she said, "the same thing brought me to their camp that led you there."

"Don't bet on it," Johnny retorted.

She tried a different tack. "Okay. The problem is, I really shouldn't tell this story to civilians, even if—"

The Blazer shuddered to a halt. Johnny pressed a button on the armrest of his door, unlocking hers. "No sweat," he told her. "You run along and file your report. We'll pick up a copy through channels."

The smile she showed him was forced, but it worked. "So, it's put out or walk? I haven't heard that one since I was a sophomore in high school."

"This isn't a date," Johnny reminded her. "And we don't have time to dance."

"There's more truth to that than you know," Ross replied. She remained in her seat and made no move to unbuckle her harness. "Another six miles, maybe seven. Turn left at the mailbox marked 'Stevens.'"

"Your cover?" asked Johnny.

"Just a squat with a comfy price tag. We've made certain improvements."

"Such as?"

"There's no roommate," she told her rescuers. "We'll have the place all to ourselves."

Their captive made a muffled sound from the Blazer's rear deck, something between a snuffle and a groan. Cooper checked him and relaxed again—or came as close to it as Ross so far had seen him manage.

These were high-strung fellows, living on the edge. She wasn't sure what drove them, who they worked for, what they wanted—but her instinct told Ross she should take a chance on trust.

For now, at least.

They rode in silence for the next five miles, until she spied a twisted tree that served as a landmark. "Next driveway on the left," she warned. "It doesn't look like much. You'll need to slow way down."

The mailbox appeared on their left, strangled by kudzu, the faded "Stevens" label barely visible between green leaves and tangled vines. At some point in the distant past the box's door had been ripped off, leaving an open maw where wasps and spiders fought for living space. It didn't matter who won out, since there'd been no mail delivered to this address for at least ten years.

It had been cheap, this house and property, purchased in a hopeless buyer's market as a "fixer-upper," by a pair of federal agents posing as husband and wife. When the present job was finished, it might serve some other purpose, but the payout from discretionary funds would not be questioned anytime soon.

Not if Ross got results.

Johnny made the turn, gravel rattling against the Blazer's undercarriage as they rolled along the narrow, curving driveway. They were soon lost to sight from the highway, their headlight beams obscured by trees and rampant undergrowth. The ramshackle house was set back a hundred yards from the road, screened by willows, concealed from passersby in darkness and barely visible in daylight even to determined searchers.

Some waddling animal, a raccoon or opossum, Ross supposed, retreated from the Blazer's headlights as they made their way toward the house. Muffled protests from their gagged companion grew more voluble, until Cooper leaned across the back seat and did something with his left hand, out of view from where Ross sat.

The noise immediately ceased.

"So, this is home?" Johnny asked her, as the headlights framed a low, ramshackle structure with a sagging porch and shingles missing from the roof.

"Just passing through," Ross answered. Her fingers found the passenger door's inside handle as Johnny braked the Blazer to an idling stop. "I'll get some light on the subject."

"I'll join you," Johnny said, sharing another glance in the rearview mirror with his companion. "Just in case there's a problem."

"Be my guest," Ross said. "I've got nothing to hide."

"I can see that," Johnny said, "from your choice of accommodations."

"Nothing to hide from you, I mean."

"Uh-huh." He didn't even try to hide his skepticism. "Let's go see about those lights."

BOLAN STOOD beside the Blazer in darkness, gun in hand, and watched dim lights go on inside the house. Drapes had been drawn across the front windows, but the light still bled through narrow gaps, illuminating random details of the cluttered, ancient porch. Waiting, he scanned the surrounding woods for shadows that appeared too mobile for the nearly windless night. He strained his ears to pick up any sounds that might be alien to the Louisiana woods at night.

Nothing.

Two minutes later, counting down the seconds in his head, he heard Johnny returning from the house. The woman who'd identified herself as Keely Ross trailed after him, a pace or two behind.

"It's clear, as far as I can tell," Johnny declared. "I couldn't scan for microphones, but I don't think there's anybody else inside."

Bolan had learned to trust his brother's judgment in such things. "Okay," he said, returning the Beretta to its holster. "Let's get this one in before he starts to make a fuss."

"There's no one else to hear him this far out from town," Ross said.

"Let's hope not," Bolan answered.

Their prisoner was conscious, but he offered no resistance as Johnny lowered the Blazer's tailgate and they pulled him out into the night. It would've been the time to make a break, if he was so inclined, but the guy made no move to escape as Bolan and Johnny led him toward the house, each gripping a muscular arm, while Ross brought up the rear. At Johnny's direction they bypassed the porch and entered through a door on the west side, into a spacious kitchen-dining room.

The place was cleaner and more modern inside than Bolan had expected. The renovators from Homeland Security, or whoever they were, had turned the place spit-and-polish, with fresh paint and brand-new appliances. From outside, the place looked ready for a wrecking ball, while inside, Bolan guessed he could probably eat off the floors.

"Want to check out the place?" the redhead asked.

"No need," Bolan said. "This should do."

The woman seemed surprised. "What, right here? In the kitchen?"

"Why not? It's close to the door, and a vinyl floor's easy to clean."

"Fair enough."

Bolan steered their captive to one of the four chairs surrounding a square dining table. The remodelers hadn't spent a fortune on furniture, and the kitchen chairs weren't built to accommodate strenuous action, but Bolan wasn't planning a prolonged interrogation. Torture ran against his grain, and he had only a few questions for their hostage. The merc could either talk, or he could die.

A simple choice.

"This won't take long," Bolan advised, as he removed the captive's gag.

"Damn right," the sullen prisoner replied. "You won't get shit from me."

"I don't need shit," the Executioner replied. "What I require from you this evening is a briefing on your mission, with the emphasis on brief."

"No way."

Bolan reached into his jacket and extracted the Beretta. "Are we clear on what's at stake?" he asked the prisoner.

"Hey, let me guess. If I don't talk, you'll shoot me in the kneecaps, then the elbows. Am I getting warm?"

"Not even close. I've never found torture reliable, and I'm not into it for sport."

"So, what's the game?"

"No game. You make a choice to live or die."

"That's pretty clear," the captive said, smiling.

"Simplicity eliminates misunderstanding."

"Do I get some time to think about it?"

Bolan shook his head. "It's now or never."

"Damn. Well, since you put it that way—"

In a flash, the prisoner erupted from his chair, hands still secured behind his back. Instead of charging Bolan's gun, he turned on Keely Ross and rushed at her, head down, plowing as if he meant to butt her through the nearest wall. Ross dodged and clipped him with an elbow on the fly, but the impact didn't even slow him. She tried to trip him, but the runner saw it coming, leaped across her out-thrust leg and veered toward the sink and the window above it. Johnny tried to tackle him, but the captive was faster. He launched himself into a dive from six feet out, clearing the sink and counter by inches, smashing his head through the windowpane into darkness.

Bolan never knew if the man truly meant to escape, or if he had planned what happened next. One burly shoulder struck the window frame and blocked his passage, dropping his throat across a jagged blade of broken glass. It sank deep into flesh and muscle, deeper still as the merc thrashed his head from side to side. Blood fountained from the gaping wound as he slid backward, rolling off the kitchen counter, to the floor.

There was no closing the wound as he lay at their feet, bleeding out; no hope of any dying declaration from his lacerated vocal cords. A trauma surgeon might have saved the captive's life, but Bolan knew the man would never make it to the Blazer, much less to some distant hospital. Implacably, he stood and watched the human sacrifice unfold.

"Jesus!" The redhead's voice was tinged with shock.

"He really didn't want to talk," Johnny observed.

"And he's still the best lead we have," Bolan said. Half-turning to face Ross, he said, "I don't suppose you knew him?"

"No such luck."

"Okay," the Executioner remarked. "Looks like we have to start from scratch."

"I'd say we start from skin," Johnny suggested, "since we have to dump the body anyway."

"No clothes, no clues." Ross sounded numb as she stared at the body with its ravaged throat and the still-expanding crimson pool.

"Your shoes," Johnny warned her.

The redhead glanced down. "They're ruined anyway," she said, but still retreated from the creeping spill of blood.

"You have a mop?" Bolan asked her.

The question seemed to snap Ross out of her trance. "In the closet," she answered, and went to fetch it, returning moments later. Without another word she got started, making frequent trips to rinse the mop in the sink.

Bolan and Johnny dragged the body clear while Ross went to work on the Red Sea. They started at the dead man's feet, while the last crimson rivulets drained from his open jugular vein and carotid artery.

He had nothing at all in any of his pockets but a black plastic comb.

He was, in short, a pro.

*We've still got fingerprints,* Johnny thought. *And DNA for sure, with all that blood.*

The U.S. military had been saving DNA samples from all personnel for nearly a decade, making sure there'd never be another Unknown Soldier. Johnny was about to give Ross a heads-up when Bolan ripped open the dead man's shirt, baring his chest.

"Well, now."

"That's custom work," Bolan said, bending closer to study the tattoo that decorated the corpse's left pectoral region. It portrayed a screaming eagle, wings spread in flight, clutching a stylized assault rifle in its talons.

Johnny squinted. "What does that say, on the eagle's breast?"

"FPP," Ross answered. She had joined them at some point, standing on the sidelines with her mop. "That's the Florida Patriot Party. It was one of the early citizen militia groups, and one of the few to survive Y2K. We've been keeping an eye on them, together with the FBI and ATF. They're suspected of arms smuggling and a couple of freelance contract murders, but so far we haven't been able to make charges stick."

Johnny caught Bolan's glance and took a gamble. "Are they Mob related?"

"It's funny you should ask." Despite her words, the redhead's frown betrayed no great amusement. "We've been picking up rumbles, the past year or so, of a possible link to the DeMitri crime Family in Miami. Does that tell you something?"

"It was just a hunch," Johnny replied.

The woman's frown deepened. "I don't think so," she challenged him. "Look, if we're working together on this—"

"Who said that?" Bolan interrupted her.

"I assumed—"

"That's mistake number one," Johnny said. "On second thought, make that two, since the other side already blew your cover."

Ross bristled. "That's a crock! I didn't tell them anything before you two came charging in—"

"To save your bacon," Johnny said.

"—to interfere. They don't know who I am or who I work for."

"If you're implying they might take you back," Bolan told her, "it's time for a major reality check."

"I didn't say that."

"You haven't said much," Johnny noted."

"Dammit! Hang on a second." Ross stormed out.

Johnny watched her leave the kitchen, moving toward the rear of the house. "Bedroom," he told Bolan.

"Did you check it for weapons?"

"I didn't have time," he admitted.

As one, they stepped away from the corpse on the floor, moving to opposite sides of the kitchen. Neither drew his pistol, but their hands were on the guns as they stood waiting. In their new positions, Ross could not tag both of them immediately if she came back shooting. One of them, at least, would be alive to take her down.

She came back with a wallet in her hand and nothing else. Noting their placement in the room, she smiled and said, "I didn't mean to make you nervous, boys."

Ross showed the wallet first to Bolan, then crossed the room and held it up for Johnny to examine. A laminated card with an unsmiling color photo identified her as Keely Mae Ross, a duly authorized agent for the United States Office of Homeland Security.

"Keely Mae?" Johnny raised his eyebrows.

"Never mind. Show me yours."

Johnny ignored the demand. "Say that's real," he told her, nodding toward the ID card. "Why should we team up with you?"

"Assuming you both pass inspection," she said, "there's the matter of pooling resources and minimizing redundancy."

"Toward what end?" Bolan asked. "We don't even know what you're working on."

"Right back at you," the lady retorted.

Johnny decided to push it. "Stalemate," he told Bolan. "I don't know about you, but I'm beat. It's past my bedtime. What say we give her custody of the stiff and call it a night?"

"Suits me," Bolan said.

He turned to Ross. "A Bureau cleanup team can help you with that blood. Good luck with the ID on your John Doe."

"Hold on!" Ross nearly stamped her foot, but caught herself before she followed through on the impulse. "This has to be negotiable."

"Not if we're working different jobs," Johnny replied.

"All right, dammit!" She took a moment, calming down. Ross spoke, her voice level, in control. "Aside from terrorism, Homeland Security deals with other threats, including violation of U.S. neutrality laws by groups or individuals. We get some static from the FBI on that, but it's our turf."

"And?" Johnny prodded.

"And we've been picking up rumbles of mercenary collusion with native rebels on a Caribbean flyspeck called Isla de Victoria. That name ring any bells?"

THEY DIDN'T HAVE to bag the dead man's hands. Keely Ross had an ink pad in one of her kitchen drawers, with a rubber stamp for her return address on bills, and she used it to roll the corpse's fingerprints onto a piece of stationery. It wasn't ideal, but from Bolan's point of view it beat hauling severed hands around in a cooler for the next few days. When she was done and the ink was dry, they faxed the prints to Stony Man Farm and to Homeland Security in Washington.

The call to Brognola, Bolan thought, could wait for morning.

While she rolled the prints, Ross told them the rest of her story. Assigned to run down the mercenary link with Maxwell Reed's Victorian Liberation Movement, she'd gone undercover as a "renegade" journalist, chasing leads from informants and classified ads in military magazines. One interview led to another, and she'd zeroed in on the camp at Bayou La-Fourche, staking out her place at the remodeled safehouse, moving in on the training facility much as Bolan and Johnny had done—but with a notable difference.

She'd been caught in the act.

"I still don't know where the guy came from," she ruefully admitted. "I was checking out a live-fire exercise, and the next thing I know, there's a gun at my head."

"When was this?" Bolan asked.

"The day before yesterday."

"And they hadn't got around to questioning you yet?" Johnny sounded surprised.

"Just the basics," Ross answered. "I went in with phony ID to explain the camera gear. They had to run a check with Wild Horizons magazine to verify my cover as a wildlife writer and photographer. I have a contact there who was supposed to back me up. Maybe they bought it. Anyway, they never brought out the thumb screws and jumper cables."

"But they were going to dump you anyway," Bolan reminded her.

A sheepish smile. "Okay. I never said the plan was flawless."

"What's your brief, from this point?" Johnny asked.

"I haven't checked in, as you know," Ross replied. "One route would be indictments for attempted murder of a federal agent."

"Bargained down to unlawful detention of a trespasser," Bolan suggested, "when you admit that you never identified yourself."

"All right. The neutrality act violations," she said. "Weapons charges. Destructive devices. I'm guessing most or all of the trainees are illegal aliens. We've got plenty to run with, I'd say."

"And if it all sticks, which I doubt," Johnny said, "you'll wind up deporting any trainees you can catch, while the in-

structors—assuming you find them at all—do six months to
a year after plea bargains."

"You sound like a lawyer," Ross told him.

Bolan looked at Johnny. "We're running short on time."

"If you're referring to Bayou LaFourche," Ross replied,
"smart money says the not-so-happy campers have already
pulled up stakes."

"I was thinking more about their landlord," Bolan said,
"and what comes after."

"Landlord?" Now the redhead looked confused. "Who's
the landlord? Am I missing something?"

"Looks like it," Johnny said. There was nothing sheepish
in his smile.

"Oh, great. I spill my guts and you give me the silent treatment. That's terrific. So professional."

"If I could get a word in edgewise—"

"He's referring to Vincent Ruggero," Bolan said.

"The gangster? You mean—?" Ross was putting the
pieces together.

"He owns Bayou LaFourche and most of the surrounding
swampland."

"Meaning he's behind the operation?"

"I suspect that's overstating it," Bolan replied. "But he's
involved, no question."

"Jesus. How'd I miss that?"

"What you see depends on where you look," Johnny reminded her.

"I'm getting that." She hesitated, then asked them, "Who
are you guys, really?"

"Our interests are the same as yours," Bolan said, "more
or less."

"What happens if I try to check that out?"

Bolan considered it, deciding Brognola could take care of

himself. "I can give you a number," he told Ross. "Your people can touch base and see what they see."

"That's nice and vague."

"Best I can do. As far as our working together, I have reservations."

"Oh, really."

"On several counts."

"Care to share them?" she asked him.

"Let's see what the brass has to say about collaboration, first. It may be immaterial."

"I may want to know, anyway." Her anger was showing.

"Your call," Bolan answered, accepting the challenge. "Two things. First, we play by different rules."

"I noticed." Ross narrowed her eyes.

"Second, I'm not sure you can cut it."

Her cheeks flamed, nearly matching the shade of her hair. "You weren't watching, I guess, in the swamp."

"I saw you defend yourself," Bolan acknowledged. "It's a whole different game, going on the offensive."

"Try me."

"Once you're in, there may not be a handy way out."

"Same answer," she said.

Bolan locked eyes with his brother, noting Johnny's shrug. "All right," he said. "Let's try it on for size. The first order of business is dumping our friend, here, before we move on."

"I can have a team come pick him up," Ross suggested.

"No good," Johnny told her. "We're off the radar now, for all intents and purposes. The fewer tracks we leave, the better it'll be for all concerned."

Ross frowned and faced Bolan. "You said we'd touch base with the brass."

"And we will," he replied. "That doesn't mean they need to know every move we make."

"Or that they want to know," Johnny added.

"Okay, then." Ross lifted her chin defiantly. "Where should we leave him?"

"That looked like a barn outside," the Executioner replied.

"It is."

"I'm guessing there's a shovel somewhere on the property."

Ross met his gaze, unflinching, standing with the body at her feet. "Let's go," she said.

**6**

## Miami

The heat was different in Miami. Stepping from the Learjet Longhorn 60's air-conditioned cabin into blazing sunlight, Vincent Ruggero knew he was too far from home. New Orleans was hot in the summer, no question, but Miami was a whole other story. It simultaneously baked and steamed, the tropical one-two punch that could put a strong man flat on his back if he wasn't accustomed to it and prepared to go the distance.

Distance.

That was the problem. Ruggero knew he should be at home, facing his problems head-on instead of leaving his capos to handle the mess, but there was too much weird shit going on.

Especially with bullets whizzing past his head.

Okay, it hadn't actually come to that, but it was too damned close for comfort when they started shooting up his tenants and their trainers in the bayou. Anybody who could pull that off and get away with it might show up in Ruggero's backyard tomorrow, lobbing munitions his way.

Besides, it wasn't all his problem, anyway.

There was plenty to go around.

A limo appeared as Ruggero stepped down from the plane. It was a stretch, so shiny-white it made him squint behind his Ray-Ban sunglasses, his mouth caught somewhere between a grimace and a smile of welcome for his host. Joey DeMitri was approaching with his hand out and his number two a measured pace behind him, on his right. Ruggero wondered if they practiced it, keeping the boss out front for a display of leadership, while making sure his ass was covered all the time.

DeMitri had a way of nodding when he talked, as if compelled to demonstrate agreement with each word he spoke. Ruggero had seen others fall into the pattern when they talked to DeMitri, five or six heads bobbing sometimes, like a flock of chickens pecking corn. Ruggero fought the tendency whenever they were face-to-face, like now.

Despite the bobbing noggin, DeMitri's grip was firm and fairly dry. How much could one hand sweat within ten paces of a limo where the a/c had to be turned up full-blast?

"Vinnie! It's good to see ya. Welcome. You remember Tom Donato? Sure ya do."

The other thing about DeMitri was his habit of fast-talking like an auctioneer.

"Sure I remember Tommy Spikes." Ruggero clasped hands briefly with the number two, each of them with their eyes concealed behind designer shades.

They entered the car, the limo's frosty air chilling Ruggero as his perspiration evaporated instantly.

"So tell me more about this shit you mentioned on the phone." DeMitri spoke before Ruggero could settle in his seat.

"The only thing I know right now," he said, "is that all hell broke loose. From what I hear, they've got a couple dozen dead. None of them were amici, though, thank God."

"Amen to that. Last thing we need's a shooting war on top of all the other shit. Too much confusion as it is, you ask me, but I went along. There's no denying it. I'd like to see some profits, though, instead of flushing money down the god-damn toilet all the time."

"Tripp says we're getting there," Ruggero said. He accepted a drink from Tommy Spikes and sipped it.

"Don't get me started on that Tripp," DeMitri warned. "Guy rubs me wrong, you wanna know the truth. Not even one of us, calling the shots like that. Too many fuckin' cooks, if you ask me. Too many fuckin' flavors."

"We voted on that, too," Ruggero reminded him.

"Don't I know it. I went along. That's what I mean. You won't hear no complaints from me. Gimme a whiskey sour, willya, Tommy? What about this paramilitary shit? Are we on top of that?"

Ruggero frowned. "Joey, I just got finished telling you—"

"We don't know anything. I heard ya, Vinnie. But I'm thinkin' maybe leaving everything to Tripp and his toy soldiers ain't the best idea we ever had. Know what I mean?"

"Go on."

"Say for example you thought someone might've followed you back here when you bailed out. What, then? Leave it to Tripp? We know this town six ways from Sunday. Who can smoke a nest of rats out any better than Tommy Spikes?"

"Damn right," Tommy agreed.

Ruggero sipped his drink. Outside, somebody slammed the limo's trunk lid down. Luggage retrieved. Frowning, Ruggero asked, "Who said they followed me?"

"Nobody. Not a soul. But think about it, Vinnie boy. What if?"

*Miami Beach*

"RELAX," Garrett Tripp said. "It's not so bad."

Despite the hotel's air-conditioning, there was a sheen of sweat on his companion's skin that made the craggy face resemble polished ebony. "Not bad? You must be joking," Maxwell Reed replied.

"I never joke about my business, Mr. President." These leaders without countries loved their titles. "And I didn't say it wasn't bad. I said it wasn't so bad. There's a difference."

"Explain, please."

"Gladly. We've lost men and some expensive gear. That's bad. We've lost Bayou LaFourche. That's also bad."

"I'm waiting for the good news, Mr. Tripp."

"Just think about it for a minute. Here we sit, with no one pounding on the door to serve a warrant. If the raid last night had been official, we'd be swimming in alphabet soup."

"Alphabet—?"

"FBI. INS. ATF. IRS. CNN. The whole gang. I've got people outside, as you know. Nothing's cooking, so far."

"So far."

"And that's good," Tripp repeated. "To see it, you have to think like the Feds. They're gung-ho, playing soldier whenever they can. They think Kevlar and goggles make them elite. They like to run clean sweeps and kick the doors in all at once."

"Which means?"

"That if it was a sanctioned operation, they'd have dragged you out of bed at the same time they were shooting up Bayou LaFourche. And that's another thing. Who ever heard of law enforcement letting suspects walk, after they've killed twenty or thirty at a crime scene? No. It's something else."

"Such as?"

"If I knew that," Tripp said, "I'd have a flying squad en route to solve the problem as we speak."

"An unknown enemy."

"A temporary situation, Mr. President. We'll find an answer and exact a fitting retribution. In the meantime, I've increased security and we're already looking for another training site. Somewhere in Mexico, perhaps, or Guatemala. I have friends in both countries who understand the value of a dollar and a secret."

"How many men were lost?" Maxwell inquired. There was a weary quality about him, as if he'd been up and worrying all night, instead of sleeping in the hotel's king-sized bed.

"The numbers aren't firm yet."

"Approximately, then. You mentioned twenty, thirty."

"It's higher," Tripp acknowledged. "In the camp, we lost fifteen for sure. Another twenty-nine were sent to chase the raiding party. We've recovered nineteen of the hunters, but the other five are likely hopeless. Alligators, quicksand…"

"Almost fifty, then. How many were my countrymen?"

"A little over half. The numbers are encouraging."

"In what bizarre philosophy?"

"As I already told you, Mr. President, the law can't walk away from that kind of engagement. They commit and stay committed."

"Am I supposed to find that comforting? You tell me that we have an enemy at large who strikes at will, kills forty men or more and fades away without a trace. You tell me it's 'good news.' I ask you again, Mr. Tripp—what are you doing to prevent a reoccurrence of this tragedy?"

"I have my men on full alert, together with our friends here in Miami and New Orleans. I've already been in touch with Bogotá, Panama City, Nassau, Calabria, Minsk and Kyoto. We've got all our ducks in a row."

"And the next attack, Mr. Tripp? How will you deal with that?"

"Superior force," Tripp said. "It's the only way to go."

"Are you suggesting that the enemy outnumbered our men last night?"

"No, sir. They took us by surprise. Our men were overconfident, and that's a fatal mistake. The survivors won't make it twice."

"I hope not, for your sake."

And yours, Tripp thought, but kept the comment to himself. He took the implied threat in stride, attributing it to Reed's nerves and the high stakes involved. Tripp recognized scare-talk when he heard it, and he didn't take it personally.

This time.

If Reed made a habit of blustering, though, there would need to be a serious adjustment in their personal relationship. Displaying forcefulness before the troops was one thing; Reed imagining he truly called the shots was something else entirely.

"We'll be ready, Mr. President," Tripp stated.

I'm ready, Tripp thought. No matter what happens.

*Washington, D.C.*

HAL BROGNOLA HAD COME to grudging terms with his office computer. They would never be friends, and he would never understand the inner workings of the machine, but there were days when he was grateful for its presence on his desk.

Like now.

The file from Aaron Kurtzman came with an attachment. Hal wasn't sure how they did that—much less how the data was encrypted to keep prying eyes from checking it out in transit—but he trusted the Stony Man crew to keep their transmissions secure. They kept some of the best brains in the business on staff to stay up to speed with cutting-edge technology for cracking codes and beating hackers at their own slick game.

This day's transmission, strictly speaking, wasn't classified. It was a dead man's personnel file, pieced together by the kind of records search that could take months or years unless a hunter knew which agencies to ask and how to phrase the crucial questions. Pull a hidden string or two, and there it was, laid out in black and white. The details of a wasted life.

The note from Kurtzman was succinct, as always: "Here's the scoop on Mr. X." But he was no longer Mr. X, now that Stony Man had done its work.

AFIS—the Justice Department's Automated Fingerprint Indexing System—had run the prints from Bolan's "John Doe" corpse in Louisiana and scored a solid hit within eighty-nine minutes of launching its search. In fact, there had been two hits, cross-referenced with details spelled out as Brognola scrolled through the document. He skimmed it first, to get the gist, then went back to the top and began to absorb the details.

Their man of mystery had once been William Alan Rogers, a.k.a. Bill Rogers, William Allen, Alan Richards and Roger Williams. The pseudonyms didn't show much imagination but they'd served him well enough in covering his tracks on several fronts while he compiled a history on both sides of the law.

"Will Rogers," Brognola muttered. "Jesus."

Their man had been born in Lodi, New Jersey, on March 26, 1971. He'd finished high school by the skin of his teeth, substandard grades and various disciplinary infractions combining to make the question of his graduation touch-and-go.

He wriggled through the academic net with some improbable scores on his final exams, but the file showed no evidence that the grades were questioned. Brognola guessed the staff was glad to see him go.

Three weeks out of high school there had been an incident with the police, auto theft bargained down to joy-riding. An old-fashioned judge gave Rogers the choice of six months in juvenile detention or two years in the Army, and Rogers had picked olive drab over jailhouse orange. In fact, he had liked the lifestyle well enough to re-up three times, for a total of eight years in service. He'd applied for Special Forces straight out of boot camp and seemingly took to the rigorous drill like a shark to salt water. Rogers had seen action in Panama, Kuwait and Somalia before he decided to hang up his green beret and strike off on his own as a soldier of fortune.

There was, of course, a back story to his decision. The year before his discharge, Rogers had been on a short list of soldiers suspected of selling stolen ordnance out of Fort Benning, Georgia. Some of the hardware had surfaced among neo-Nazis plotting a race war in Mobile; the rest was still missing. There hadn't been sufficient evidence to charge any of the suspects, but heat from the FBI and the Army's Criminal Investigation Division would've been nerve-racking after a while. Rogers took his discharge, left a phony forwarding address and dropped out of sight.

His trail got hazy from there, though Kurtzman's team had found enough landmarks to persuade the big Fed that they were on the right track. Under one name or another, Rogers had dirtied his hands with gunrunning to Colombia, drug trafficking from Mexico and a suspected contract murder in Seattle. On the "straight" side of the mercenary ledger, he had been reported active on the firing line in Peru, Sri Lanka,

Rwanda and East Timor. If the reports were true, he had multiple passports, since State Department records couldn't track him any farther than Mexico City, in 1999.

The stateside crimes of which he was suspected told Brognola that Rogers had to know someone—and probably several someones—in organized crime. Amateurs didn't walk into big drug or arms deals with any prospect of surviving the transaction. Beyond the basic nickel bag or Saturday-night special, that kind of traffic required connections. Just like setting up a mercenary training camp on land owned by a ranking member of the Mafia.

Brognola needed more if he was going to feed Bolan a live target, instead of simply telling tales about the dead. Then he came to the phone logs. Rogers had dialed one number repeatedly over the past year and a half. The number matched a name, and the name had yet another file attached.

Before he finished reading through the second dossier, the big Fed knew they'd found a hook.

*Baton Rouge, Louisiana*

THEY DON'T MAKE phone booths like they used to. Wayland Spade had never seen a proper walk-in phone booth in the flesh, but they cropped up in films from time to time. It pissed him off that modern public telephones were mounted on walls with a slim metal ledge underneath, too small for taking notes on any paper larger than an index card, and a plastic hood barely large enough to keep rain off the telephone itself while the caller got soaked.

Stingy bastards.

It was drizzling. Warm water soaked through Spade's jacket and ran down the back of his neck, but he was used to shitty weather. It came with the paycheck. He was more concerned about an incoming call than the raindrops plastering thin stands of sandy hair across his freckled scalp.

Two minutes.

Tripp was never late.

Spade picked up on the first ring, never one for playing hard to get. Tripp didn't care for games, and this was definitely not the time to get him started.

"What's the latest?" Tripp demanded without preamble.

Spade grimaced. "Nothing new, so far."

Tripp's voice went colder than normal, a dip into Arctic waters. "How can that be?"

"We've got nothing to work with," Spade answered. "They rented a boat and we sweated the owner, but it's a dead end. He took cash from two guys, 'normal-looking' he tells me. They dropped the boat off overnight and took off. He never saw them again."

"He's a problem," Tripp observed.

"Not any more." Unless the old man gave some alligator indigestion.

"What about the woman?"

Scowling, Spade replied, "She's definitely gone. That doesn't mean she's still alive, but—"

"We can't trust dumb luck at this stage of the game," Tripp said, cutting him off. "My understanding is that you learned nothing from her."

"We were close."

"Meaning it's a washout. Now she's gone, we don't know who she was or who came in to extricate her."

"Maybe she's a writer, like she claimed." It sounded lame, even as he said it, but Spade had to say something.

"A writer with friends who could pull this kind of stunt to help her, killing forty-odd men in the process? Dream on."

"They got lucky, all right?"

"There's no such thing as luck. There's preparation, and there's negligence. They were ready. You weren't."

"I'll fix it," Spade promised.

"I'm counting on it," Tripp replied. "This kind of screw-up is the last thing we need right now. There's too much riding on this deal. The money men won't stand for it. Neither will I."

Spade knew what that meant. "Whoever ran this down, it had to be a private op," he said. "We'd be ass-deep in warrants, otherwise."

"So, tell me something I don't know."

"I'm thinking someone on the money side may know more than they're letting on. These guys have enemies to spare, including military types from half a dozen countries. Maybe you should talk to them."

"It's in the works," Tripp said. "Meanwhile, your job is following the scent. Two men or twenty, they can't disappear without a trace—at least until I've had a chance to question them."

"I'm working on it," Spade repeated.

"Work harder. Get it done. There's no place in this operation for a soldier who can't pull his weight."

The line went dead. Spade listened to the droning dial tone for a moment, mouthed a curse and cradled the receiver. All at once, he felt the rain again.

*I pull my fucking weight,* he thought. *You bet your ass.*

Now all he had to do was prove it, before Tripp suddenly decided that his number two was expendable. There would be no appeal from that decision, and no advance warning.

To save himself, Spade had to find the enemy.

But where in hell should he begin to look?

*Baldwin County, Alabama*

THEY CHOSE A TRUCK STOP fifteen miles east of Mobile, where he pay phones were mounted outside and the parking lot held enough vehicles for one more to pass without drawing attention. This was the sort of Deep South region where a "Yankee" license plate still raised some hoary eyebrows, and the last thing Bolan needed at the moment was a nosy sheriff's deputy sniffing around the Blazer with its cargo of hardware and secrets.

They'd done well so far, driving around the clock in shifts, one or another of them sleeping as fatigue kicked in. Pensacola was thirty-odd miles due east of the truck stop, and from there it was a mere 673 miles to Miami. Call it ten hours and change, with two more pit stops for the Blazer.

It rankled Bolan to give his targets that much lead time, but driving meant ready access to vital equipment, plus no ambush waiting in a crowded airport terminal. The other side knew Keely Ross's face, if nothing more, but spotting her on wheels in tourist-infested Florida would be the next thing to impossible. Delay would also give the enemy a chance to think the raid on Bayou LaFourche was a fluke. They'd be running in circles, trying to figure it out, any optimists among them pushing the "isolated incident" scenario—until the second shoe dropped.

Let them wait.

While Johnny filled the Blazer's tank and Ross ordered food to go, Bolan had a call to make. He rang through to Washington, watching passersby and keeping his comments to a minimum while Brognola ran down the personal history of the late merc. There was nothing in the tawdry saga calculated to spark any feelings of sympathy for William Alan Rogers.

Bolan thanked Brognola for the information, passed on their presumed itinerary and broke the connection. He got back to the Blazer just as Ross returned with three foam boxes and a six-pack of cola.

They ate their burgers on the move, Johnny driving one-handed. Between mouthfuls, Bolan briefed them on the dead man's background and his constant phone calls to the Sunshine State.

"Same number all the time?" Ross asked.

"A David Packham in Fort Lauderdale," Bolan replied.

"Who's that?" Johnny asked.

Ross didn't wait for Bolan to supply the answer. "Head honcho in the Florida Patriot Party," she said. "He calls himself 'Colonel' Packham these days, but he never got beyond lance corporal in the Marine Corps, before they cut him a bad-conduct discharge in 1987. Drunk and disorderly conduct, combined with extremist activity in his free time. He's been drifting around the far right ever since, checking out various groups, including the Klan. When the militia movement came along, he saw a chance to mix business with paranoid pleasure. Most of the groups in that wave have collapsed, but Packham's managed to retain a couple hundred die-hard devotees."

"You knew they were involved with Isla de Victoria?" Johnny asked.

"Not until I heard the stats on Rogers. Even so, the FPP may not be down with Maxwell Reed. The bayou may've been a fill-in gig for Rogers. Even patriots need to pay rent and put gas in the Humvee."

"You mentioned a Klan connection to the Florida Patriots?" Bolan asked.

"Nothing solid. Some of the Patriots are kluckers—or were, before they saw the light with Packham. It's not a white supremacist movement per se, though I'd bet you my pension that most of them think every step toward equality since 1860 was part of some Communist plot."

"Would that bar them from working with Reed?" Johnny asked.

Ross considered it for a moment, then shook her head.

"I doubt it. If you read their literature, their main fear is something they call 'One-World Government.' They're convinced the collapse of the Soviet Bloc was a sham to throw us off guard. The color that scares them most is red, not black."

"And most of them are military vets?" Johnny asked.

"All but a handful of kooks and cling-ons," she replied.

"So there's nothing to stop them from signing on to help a bunch of 'freedom fighters' liberate some tropic paradise."

"Nothing at all when you put it that way."

"Okay," Bolan said. "Since Fort Lauderdale was on our glide path anyway, why don't we stop and have a parley with the patriots?"

"COME IN, TOMMY, and have a seat. Something to drink?"

"No thanks, boss," Tommy Spikes replied. "I'm good."

"We've got a situation."

"Don Ruggero's mess."

"Not strictly his." Joey DeMitri was a strong believer in accepting personal responsibility, as long as it was relatively painless and the price tag wasn't out of line. "We have a stake in this thing too. You know that."

"Sure, boss. But the whole Louisiana end is his. My thinking is, he dropped the ball and let it get away from him."

"Let's say you're right. As members of the team, what do we do about it?"

"Well—"

"We need to find out who's behind this thing and take them out before they do more damage, yes?"

"Right, boss."

"So, how tough can it be?"

"I'd say no sweat, if we were looking for these guys in

Florida. But Louisiana is Ruggero's territory. He's got the connections there, not us."

"Lucky for us he's come to visit, then," DeMitri replied.

"You think?" It took another second for Tommy Spikes to catch on. "Oh, since he's here, you think the guys'll try to find him?"

"You got it."

"And since this is our turf, we should have no problem taking care of them."

DeMitri smiled. "So, you're on it, then?"

Tommy Spikes got the hint and came out of his chair. "Right away, boss. Full alert." He made it to the door, then paused with one hand on the knob. "We don't have anything like a description, I suppose?"

"That's where you need to work your magic, Tommy."

"Right. No sweat."

The door banged shut behind the capo, leaving Joey De-Mitri to consider his dilemma. It was possible that nothing would bleed over to his territory from the trouble in Louisiana, but he didn't have much faith in miracles. Unless Ruggero had an enemy who knew his business inside out, the raid on Garrett Tripp's facility could only mean that some aspect of their collaborative venture was exposed. Not just exposed, but under fire.

And that meant trouble all around.

An adversary who could link Ruggero with the operation might be able to connect the dots between Louisiana and Miami. And it might not be enough for him to kick the hell out of some revolutionary wanna-bes outside of Baton Rouge. An enemy like that would probably want more.

But looking for his payoff on DeMitri's turf would be the worst mistake he ever made.

The last fucking mistake.

Joey DeMitri had clawed his way up from the streets of Brooklyn to become a made man, then fought every color of would-be Godfather Miami could muster to win himself a place in the sun. He wasn't about to relinquish it now, on the verge of great things, just because Vinnie Ruggero let some hotshot gunners waltz into his territory and raise hell with the hired help.

It was Garrett Tripp's problem, as much as anyone else's, and while DeMitri had already received Tripp's assurances of "remedial action" in progress, that didn't mean DeMitri was bound to sit back and watch strangers defend his territory.

**7**

*Fort Lauderdale*

The next best thing to long nights on a mission, Otis Poole decided in the hazy hour of 4:30 a.m., was any night devoted to pursuit of alcohol and getting laid. But it was only better if the hunt turned out to be successful.

No problem on the juice, since he could buy that anywhere, at any hour of the day or night. The other could be a problem, however, and there had been too many goddamn nights when Poole had come home from the hunt well-lubed but empty-handed, fit for nothing but collapsing in his lonely, unmade bed.

Poole shied away from outright hookers most times, and he had a certain standard for the women he graced with his favors. Lately, the past five years or so, he'd found the numbers thinning out a bit. Not women who attracted him, but those who would encourage him to follow through.

When he was halfway sober and alone, like now, Poole wondered if his style was going out of style.

Hell, no, he told himself, slapping the Bronco's steering wheel for emphasis. How could that be? He was a self-employed jack-of-all-trades who made the better part of thirty grand some years, off the books most of it, and he owned his single-wide mobile home outright. Same for the four-year-old Bronco, though he'd fallen a bit behind on the insurance payments of late. Damn rules and regulations were all part of the conspiracy to strangle freedom in America, so why the hell should he care?

Unless he got stopped some night, doing eighty in a sixty-five with liquor on his breath.

Oh, well.

If women couldn't recognize a white Christian patriot when they saw one, that was their problem. A short way down the road, when they were faced with The Collapse and everything they knew went straight to hell in a hand basket, some would be anxious to know the Supreme Commander of the Florida Patriot Party. Who else would help them when "polite society" began to fall apart?

The ladies would be flocking to his doorstep then, and begging Poole to take them in.

This night didn't count anyway, he decided. Poole was still in shock about the news from Baton Rouge. Bill Rogers and a mess of others were either blown away or missing in the swamps out there, done in by God knew who. He thought about some of their training sessions in the Glades and knew that dying in a swamp at night was a brutal way to go.

Poole didn't know how the Louisiana business would rebound on him, but Tripp had told him not to sweat it. Just a glitch, he'd said. Stay cool and keep your mouth shut. As if Poole was given to disclosing secrets to civilians, drunk or sober.

Not a frigging chance.

He didn't know that much about the operation anyway, aside from dealing guns to Tripp and getting updates from

Rogers on how they were coming along with their training. It wasn't an FPP operation to start with, just a chance to make some money under the table while tossing a monkey wrench into the Red world-enslavement machine.

And why not?

Opportunity didn't come knocking that often in Poole's neighborhood.

Poole was braking for his driveway when saw the woman. Saw her ass, would be more like it, and decided on the spot that he'd seen none to match it in the past eight hours. It was aimed directly at his headlights, sheathed in skintight faded denim, as she stared beneath the raised hood of a two-door Japanese sedan.

Poole pulled his Bronco onto the gravel shoulder, parking so his headlights framed the woman and her car. She turned to face him, one hand raised to shade her eyes and looking worried. Strangers stopping on the road at night to "help" might be another kind of trouble worse than engine failure, and that knowledge was reflected in the pinched expression on her face.

Still pretty though, he noticed. Nice red hair. A slim, athletic build as far as he could tell. And just a bit top-heavy in that low-cut T-shirt she was wearing, which was fine with Poole. The only object in her hands appeared to be a small flashlight in some designer color, maybe purple or maroon.

Poole was already smiling as he stepped down from the driver's seat. He left the Bronco's engine running, for the lights. "Looks like you got a bit o' trouble, ma'am," he said.

"It just quit on me," she replied. "I don't know why. There's half a tank of gas, I swear!"

"It happens," Poole assured her. "I can take a look, if you want me to. If I can't fix it, there's an all-night station back the way I come from, six or seven miles. I'll give you a lift down there on your say-so."

"Honestly?" She cracked a winning smile. "I'd be forever grateful."

Not forever, Poole amended. Just tonight. He put a little extra wattage on his grin and said, "Sounds fair to me."

The plain truth was that while Poole knew his way around a toolbox well enough to change the Bronco's oil, replace the air filter or bleed the radiator, when it came to fixing cranky engines he was groping in the dark. He'd never tell a woman that, of course, particularly when he planned on groping her as part of his reward for playing good Samaritan.

"I'm afraid it's beyond me," he told her after some useless tinkering. "You want to, we can take that ride down to the station, see if the mechanic's got a vacancy."

"The ride sounds good," she said, "but you're all the mechanic I'll be needing."

Poole was trying to think of an answer, wondering if he'd dozed at the wheel and dreamed himself into one of those letters from Penthouse, when a pair of strong arms grabbed him from behind and the mother of all mosquitoes sank its lance into the left side of his neck.

Poole tried to struggle, kicking backward at his unseen enemy and glaring at the woman, but he seemed to have no strength. Her image blurred and ran before his drooping eyes. A moment later, Otis Poole was snoring like a baby in the deep, warm dark.

*Miami*

"By ALL MEANS tell His Excellency that the new security force is in place and ready to insure his safety." Garrett Tripp listened to the anxious voice in his ear and replied, "No, they may not be visible. That's why we call it security. If the opposition appears, they walk into a trap."

More babble in his ear, the singsong voice.

He signed off pleasantly then dropped the receiver into its cradle, drew a deep breath and exhaled his frustration with Maxwell Reed's aides. The would-be president of Isla de Victoria was bad enough, but his hangers-on could drive a sober man to drink.

Speaking of which…

It was beer-o'clock somewhere on Earth, Tripp supposed, and since it was still dark outside, he could pretend it was night instead of morning. Why not? He'd never thought much of the rules imposed on self-indulgent behavior by people who didn't indulge. Tripp knew his limits, and his private discipline was ironclad. He never drank or did anything else to excess.

Well, maybe one thing.

But he wouldn't have a chance to scratch that itch unless the unknown enemy revealed himself.

Tripp was reaching inside the fridge when the telephone rang. He left the beer where it was and walked back to the counter, unruffled by calls at this ungodly hour.

"Tripp-Wire Security."

"You recognize my voice?"

"Of course I do, Mr. DeMitri."

"Hey! I hope this line's secure," the mobster protested.

"I check it for taps twice a day," Tripp replied. "Can I help you with something?"

"That's my question, hotshot. You know I've got company here, since your boys dropped the ball on the bayou. I'm hoping there won't be any kinda instant replay on that fuckup, if you get my drift."

"I'm way ahead of you," Tripp said. And wasn't that God's honest truth? "I have extra security in place on our mutual friend, and more people expected this morning. If you need any help—"

"We're good here," DeMitri said. "I'm just checking in to make sure you got all your ducks in a row."

"We'll be ready," Tripp promised. "Of course, it would help if you gave me a list of your guest's enemies."

"I'll ask around. Meanwhile, I think we can assume the hit had more to do with our thing in the islands than business at home."

"I don't get paid to make assumptions," Tripp replied. "You want the bases covered, that to me means all the bases."

"Hey, I said I'd ask. What do you know about the woman?" DeMitri asked.

"Other than the fact she's disappeared, nothing."

"She could be the reason for the blow-up, right?"

"I wouldn't rule out anything at this point," Tripp said. "I'll do my best to get some answers.

"Do better, hotshot. Last I heard, your best fell short."

The line went dead before Tripp could respond. He smoldered for a moment, then dismissed the feeling. Joey DeMitri wasn't his problem right now. Not yet.

But someday soon, perhaps.

No insults forgotten, no favors unrepaid.

They were words to live by—or to die by, as the case may be.

And Tripp never forgot anything.

JOHNNY GRAY KNEW from firsthand experience that it was embarrassing to wake up naked in a strange place, with little or no idea of where he was or how he got there. It had happened once or twice in college, but the young ladies who woke up with him always made the trip worthwhile.

He had to guess how it would feel, waking nude in a strange place, bound hand and foot to a cold metal chair.

Their hostage was living the nightmare right now.

"Whu…whu…where…? What the hell?"

"Save your breath," Johnny told him. "You'll need it to answer some questions."

The prisoner had questions of his own, however. "Where am I?" he demanded. "What's this all about? Who the fuck are you people?"

"I'll give you those three, since you're still confused," Johnny replied. "You're in a safe place, nice and private. You're about to take a quiz where you're life depends on the answers. And we're the people who decide if you pass or fail."

The hostage looked around, still groggy. Most of the cavernous warehouse was lost in shadows, a single bank of light fixtures beaming overhead. It took another moment for him to recognize Keely Ross on the sidelines and make the connection. Anger flared in his face.

"You're the bitch who set me up! If I wasn't tied up to this chair—"

"You'd do what, big boy?" Ross challenged. Then, with a glance toward the prisoner's lap, she added, "No, I guess we shouldn't call you that."

Thrashing at his bonds, Poole nearly tipped the chair. He settled down when Bolan and Johnny each stepped closer, and he saw the pistols slung beneath their arms.

"You gonna kill me then, or what?" he asked petulantly.

"If we wanted you dead, you'd be dead," Johnny answered. "I told you, we want information."

"Name, rank and serial number," Poole said. He tried to flex his muscles, but his bonds made it a wasted effort.

Poole glanced down at the concrete floor. His chair was planted in the middle of a puddle roughly ten feet wide. "What's this?" he asked.

"It's a little difficult to see from your position," Johnny explained, "but we've removed the rubber caps from the legs of your chair."

"What the hell?"

"Just making sure," Johnny said.

"Sure of what?"

"That you're a well-grounded individual."

"What's that supposed to mean?"

Bolan silently retreated from the sphere of light, returning moments later with a mover's dolly, rolling on fat rubber tires. A red hand-crank generator was strapped to the dolly, black jumper cables with gleaming alligator clips draped over the top of its casing. Poole recoiled from the sight—or would have, if he'd been able to move.

"This is all a mistake," he declared.

"If it is, we'll find out soon enough," Johnny said.

"I never saw you folks before today. I don't know anything about you, dammit!"

"That's okay, Stubby," Ross said. "We don't need any info on ourselves."

"What, then?" Poole's eyes were riveted on Bolan as he set about untangling the generator's cables, snapping the heavy-duty clips.

"You had a friend named William Alan Rogers," Johnny said, not making it a question.

"Billy, sure." If Poole had picked up on the past tense, he was choosing to ignore it.

"He's been calling you long-distance from Louisiana."

"Now and then. So what?"

"Smart money says you're tied in with the people he was working for," Ross said.

"You'd lose that bet," Poole said. "It was a private thing of Billy's."

"You just let your soldiers wander off and do their own

thing as they please, no kickbacks to the party?" Johnny frowned and shook his head. "No sale, Otis."

For emphasis, Bolan gave the generator's handle three swift turns and Johnny brought the alligator clips together, white fire crackling between them for an instant.

"Don't do this!" Poole whimpered.

"You're not leaving me a choice," Johnny replied. "We need that information, even if it takes all night."

"Five minutes, tops," Ross interjected.

"Okay! Just put that thing away!"

"It stays right here until we're satisfied," Johnny said.

"I didn't have no part in any of the training, I swear to Jesus. But I helped them with some hardware when they had a little shortage, some months back."

"What kind of hardware?" Johnny asked him.

"Nothin' special. Just some rifles, clips and ammunition, stuff like that. We got a man in Jacksonville, at the Navy Air Depot. He's good for things like that from time to time."

"That's close enough," Johnny said. "All we need now is the name and address of your contact on the other side."

"Jesus, he'll kill me sure as shit if I do that," Poole wailed.

Bolan leaned in close to let the hostage see his eyes and asked, "What makes you think we won't?"

*Miami*

"THERE'S STILL no word?" DeMitri asked.

Vincent Ruggero felt a sour rumbling in his stomach. "Nothing," he said. "I would've told you if they found out anything."

"Of course, I understand." DeMitri made it sound so reasonable, sitting over coffee while the maid cleared off their breakfast plates. "It's just a funny thing, ya know?"

"Tell me about it, eh?" Ruggero didn't feel like covering

the same old ground again, but common sense told him his
host was not about to let it rest. "I've got my people on the
street, working every lead they can find—which so far means
none at all. Connections in the state police and sheriff's office, same damn thing. The Feds get into it, I've got more
trouble than a few dead boat people, if you know what I
sayin'."

"Our friend Tripp was askin' me this morning," DeMitri
said, "whether you had any old competitors or enemies
floatin' around out there, who might've done this thing."

"You kiddin' me?" Ruggero had to laugh, despite his
sour mood. "Who's gonna come at me this way, through
this thing in the islands? Who even knows, outside the
Family?"

DeMitri hunched forward, leaning on his elbows. "You
want the whole list? Come on, Vinnie, get real! We got partners in this thing all over the planet, for Christ's sake."

"They're partners, okay? Who'd wanna bitch it up to get
at me? I don't know most of them from Adam, and the others—the Colombians, for instance—we've been doin' business right along, without a hitch."

"I didn't mean one of the inside people," DeMitri explained. "All those players, though, there's bound to be a leak
somewhere. Somebody knows our business when they ain't
supposed to."

"I was counting Tripp's people for security out there,"
Ruggero said, fuming. "He dropped the fucking ball, and
now he acts like it's no big deal, ya know?"

"That's how it is with soldiers," DeMitri said. "They don't
get emotional."

"Another fuck-up like the last one, and he'll get emotional
all right. I'll see to that myself."

"Don't get yourself worked up there, Vinnie." There

was something off about DeMitri's smile. Ruggero couldn't put his finger on it, but he didn't like his host's expression.

"What the hell? Don't get worked up? I'm sittin' here, a god-damn fugitive, when I should be at home and taking care of business. You're climbing up my ass for answers every couple hours, and you tell me not to get worked up? You think maybe I oughta laugh it off and spend a few days working on my tan?"

"I think you need to recognize when you've done every-thing you can, then let it go. Sit back and wait, like you were in a duck blind with your shotgun. We'll have targets com-ing up before you know it, Vinnie. Trust me. I can feel it."

"We'd better have some goddamn targets, Joey." There was spring-steel in Ruggero's voice and murder in his eyes. "Be-cause I'm sick to death of playing hide-and-seek."

"No problem," DeMitri said. "We're about to change the rules."

Ruggero sipped his coffee, making no reply, but he was still uneasy with DeMitri's tone. He'd have to watch Miami's Don more closely in the days ahead, make sure DeMitri didn't have a secret plan in place to cut Ruggero out and grab a larger slice of pizza for himself.

God help anyone who tried to take advantage of Vinnie Ruggero.

"HE'S NERVOUS, then," Tommy Spikes said.

"Nervous, embarrassed—call it what you want." DeMitri fanned the air dismissively with one manicured hand. "He knows he dropped the ball. Now we have to try and save the game ourselves. I'm thinking we should get a little somethin' extra on our end for all the trouble."

Tommy knew what that meant, and it made him nervous.

"Whose gonna give us that?" Tommy Spikes asked cautiously. It didn't pay to piss off Joey, especially when he was in a mood, like now.

DeMitri frowned at the question, but he didn't explode. "We're not the only ones involved in this thing," he replied. "The others see we're doin' more than our share of the work, carryin' twice the load, they'll come across. You wait and see."

Tommy wasn't convinced, but he knew better than to argue with the Don. He didn't know about the Asian players, but the Colombians and Russians weren't well-known for their negotiating skills, much less their generosity. If there was a division in the stateside ranks, Tommy suspected they might turn and try to grab the whole thing for themselves.

"You got some different thoughts on this?"

DeMitri's voice snapped Tommy Spikes back to the here and now. He realized that he'd been drifting. "Not me, boss," he lied. "I think you're right."

About Ruggero blowing it, at least. A Don who let strangers blitz through his territory at will was riding for a fall, no question. As to whether the Miami Family could profit from the situation, however, Tommy Spikes was not at all convinced.

"I count on your advice. You know that don'tcha, Tommy?"

"Sure thing, Joey."

"Maybe you're thinking Vinnie's stronger than he looks, right now."

Tommy was thinking that, in fact. And he was also thinking that the guys who raised so much hell in Louisiana might come looking for a little taste in Florida. If that turned out to be the case, Tommy was thinking a united front might serve them better than a house divided.

"You'd know more about his strength than I do, Joey," Tommy said, wondering if that were really true.

"You're right," DeMitri stated. "Right on the money. I've got eyes inside Ruggero's Family. He doesn't make a move without me knowin' it."

The smile felt strange on Tommy's face. "That's good to hear. You wanna take him, then?"

"Not yet. We'll wait a while and see what happens first. If there's no trouble on our end, I'll wait a couple days and send him home to clean his house. We catch a piece of what blew up on Vinnie's end, we'll need to talk again."

"Sounds good."

"Meantime, what's shakin' on security?"

"I called in all our people, plus a couple dozen guys from Sammy Stein."

"That's good. We keep the lid on nice and tight, maybe we don't have any trouble and the problem with our good friend from New Orleans goes away. But if it doesn't, Tommy, I'll be countin' on ya."

Tommy Spikes produced a smile from somewhere, holding it in place until his cheeks went numb.

THE SAFEHOUSE WAS a bungalow in Hialeah, northwest of Miami proper. Bolan wasn't sure who owned it—possibly the FBI or DEA, but there were at least half a dozen other acronym agencies working the district on behalf of federal, state and local authorities. What Bolan cared about was privacy, including front and backyards screened by trees and shrubbery, with a detached garage toward the rear of the property, reached by a sixty-foot driveway. The bungalow itself featured three bedrooms, two baths, a small living room and a combination kitchen-dining room. The swimming pool out back was empty, carpeted with dead leaves.

A car was waiting for them in the small garage, keys underneath a floor mat on the driver's side. It was a Lexus LS

400, no doubt confiscated from some dealer on his way to the joint. No state or federal agency had purchased those luxury wheels off the showroom floor.

They sat around the kitchen table, nursing mugs of coffee and jawboning strategy. The information gleaned from Otis Poole had given them a target. Two targets, to be more precise. One was a mercenary named Wayland Spade, whom Keely Ross identified as the top-ranking soldier at Bayou LaFourche. Unfortunately, Spade's whereabouts were unknown at the moment, which left them with target number two.

The other mark was Eddie Licavoli, a subcapo in Joseph DeMitri's Miami crime Family. He was the link Bolan needed to tie up loose ends, a tangible connection between the Mob-merc collaborative effort in Louisiana and South Florida, with easy access to the Caribbean. Maxwell Reed was just a few miles up the road, in Fort Lauderdale.

So far, the pieces fit.

But Bolan's gut told him the puzzle was still incomplete.

A large-scale map of Dade County covered most of the table's surface. Resting near its center, slightly larger than a normal piece of typing paper, was a detailed sketch of Joseph DeMitri's Miami estate, located just off Dixie Highway, a few miles southwest of the Orange Bowl stadium. They didn't have a floor plan for the house itself, but federal spotters had done a good job with their overflights of the property.

"Two acres, give or take," Bolan said. "We can assume that it's guarded and features security gear besides the closed-circuit TV cameras marked on the sketch."

Those were spotted along the estate's outer wall at two hundred-foot intervals, four more red-inked at each corner of the massive three-story house.

"That's a lot to get past," Ross remarked.

"If they're on when we try it," Johnny said.

"Meaning?"

Johnny leaned across the table, tapping a point on the sketch, near the northeast corner of DeMitri's property. "Neutralize this utility pole," he told Ross, "and we black out half the neighborhood, including security systems. There's nothing on the diagram to indicate a backup generator. Even if the cameras have battery backup, the grounds should be dark."

"I don't know about this," she said, shaking her head.

Bolan understood the agent's reservations. Fighting in the swamp had been pure self-defense. They were changing the rules now, and Ross would be crossing the line. Nothing she saw or did in the night ahead could be described in court without making herself a defendant on multiple felony charges.

"You talked to your people, right?" Johnny prodded.

"That's right."

"And they gave you the green light."

"They told me to use my best judgment," she answered. "It's not the same thing."

"Plausible deniability," Bolan said. "They're giving you enough rope to hang yourself, without implicating headquarters."

"I figured that out for myself. I'm not sure I can do it."

"It's time to get sure," Bolan told her, "or bow out of the game."

"You'd like that, wouldn't you?" she challenged.

"Depends on whether you can handle it," the Executioner replied. "We'll have enough to do tonight, without hauling deadweight."

"It wouldn't hurt to have a driver waiting, though," Johnny chimed in.

Bolan considered it. "You'd still be on the wrong side of the law," he said.

Ross frowned, then inhaled deeply.

"Okay," she said, exhaling. "I'm in."

**8**

Johnny Gray, black-clad from head to steel-capped toe and painted for the night, crouched in a bank of shrubbery against the northwest flank of Joey DeMitri's walled estate. The weapon clutched against his Kevlar-padded chest was an H&K MP-5 SD-3 submachine gun, the folding-stock model with a factory-installed suppressor. If noise were required, he had a Glock 22 on his hip, loaded with the same Smith & Wesson .40-caliber rounds mandated for FBI side arms, and a mixed bag of grenades suitable for all occasions.

Johnny's wristwatch, synchronized with the others', told him that the charges would blow in another two minutes and seventeen seconds. He'd given himself an extravagant fifteen minutes to descend the utility pole and hit his mark, just in case a prowl car dawdled past and left him hanging. But now he was in place and champing at the bit.

His brother was as calm as death, at least on the outside, and Johnny rarely caught a glimpse of what was happening within. As for Ross, he didn't know her well enough to read her moods, much less her mind, but in stray moments since their meeting he'd found himself wishing they had some spare time to get to know each other.

She'd jumped at the chance to drive getaway, and Johnny had been relieved that they wouldn't be cutting her loose just yet. But that could all go sour in a heartbeat if Ross decided to betray them—or if she simply got spooked and took off without her passengers when the fireworks started.

Johnny huddled in darkness, smelling gun oil, juniper and fresh-mown grass. He waited, watching streetlights down the way and counting off the seconds in his head.

Another fifty…forty-five…forty…

He braced himself, ready to leap and scale the wall, testing his leather gloves and rip-stop uniform against its crown of razor wire. Whatever else the wire might do to him, it wouldn't fry him with a lethal voltage.

Not if they were right about the backup generator.

The detonation didn't sound like much, but Johnny felt a hot rush of excitement as the neighborhood went dark. Rising, he swung the MP-5 around behind him, toward the middle of his back, and leaped to grab the wall's upper lip, toes digging against cinder blocks. It was nothing compared to the obstacle courses he'd beaten in Ranger training, and nothing compared to the swamp where he'd fought for his life two nights earlier.

The razor wire nipped him but didn't bite deep. Johnny shielded his face and rolled clear of the tangle, dropping into a crouch amidst ferns and more shrubs at the base of the wall.

He was in.

Mack, too, he supposed, barring some unforeseen complication. His headset was silent, but that was expected. They both knew their jobs and had no need to chat. Outside, in the Lexus, Ross had one job and one only: to stay alert and respond on demand when they began their withdrawal.

Johnny started for the house, navigating through darkness by the sound of raised, angry voices. DeMitri's security people might not be afraid of the dark, but they didn't relish it, either. Clutching his SMG with the safety off, Johnny jogged toward the sound.

Any minute now, they'd learn to fear the dark.

It was a lesson some of them might live to remember.

TOMMY SPIKES HAD EARNED his nickname at age twenty-one, when he donned a pair of golf shoes and stomped a pair of Cuban contract killers into bloody pulp before an audience of thirteen ranking Mafiosi. That was the night he took his oath, and there had been no looking back. But Tommy still had fleeting doubts about his choice from time to time.

Like now, for instance.

Standing in the dark and waiting for some flunky to retrieve a flashlight, Tommy Spikes wished he was anywhere but standing guard over DeMitri and Ruggero when the lights went out.

Because this felt like a hit.

He had nothing to prove it yet, but Tommy Spikes knew the feeling. The flashlight was barely in his hand before he started snapping orders at the soldiers still remaining with him in DeMitri's study.

"Break out the guns, Eddie," he commanded, watching Licavoli move toward the closet that concealed a gun vault. "Hardware all around. Benny and Chuck, soon as you're strapped, I need you on the grounds, checking your buttons. Cheech, you got the house. Nobody but *amici* in or out, unless I give the word."

A chorus of assent came back at him, but Tommy Spikes wasn't listening. He took the first gun handed through the door, moving toward the hallway while his men scrambled to grab guns and follow.

*Better ready than caught with our pants down*, he thought,

as he emerged from the room, flashlight in one hand, shotgun in the other. He heard raised voices, muffled by walls and distance, Joey DeMitri's grating tones still recognizable in spite of everything.

A night like this, Tommy thought, Don Ruggero could have himself an accident and no one would think twice about it. Well, that wasn't true. New Orleans would think twice and then some, but what could they prove? If it wasn't an accident after all, maybe the hit was pulled off by whoever chased Ruggero out of his home territory, chewing up the scenery back there.

Something to think about, Tommy Spikes told himself, but it would be a damned risky business, pulling off a hit like that on his own initiative, without DeMitri's sanction and support.

He was still skulling over that notion when the shooting started somewhere on the grounds outside. An automatic weapon stuttered, once and then again, before a symphony of small arms rang out in the night.

A fucking hit. I knew it!

He was running then, and shouting at the other men to follow him. "Come on, goddammit! This is it! You heroes get to earn your pay!"

THE FIRST KILL WAS practically silent, only a muffled grunt as Bolan slipped his left arm around the careless sentry's throat and the crunch as he twisted hard to the left, snapping the young man's neck. The sentry shivered once, then went slack in his arms.

Bolan was backing toward a large oak tree, planning to hide the body in its shadow, when a startled voice demanded, "What the fuck is this?"

The Executioner turned toward the voice as the new arrival raised a submachine gun, sighting down the stubby barrel. It looked like an Uzi or one of those knockoffs produced in half a dozen countries from Poland to Argentina. Bolan used the dead man as a shield when the second sentry opened up, taking the hits and reeling backward while he swung his sound suppressed CAR-15 into target acquisition.

The SMG rattled off a second burst, this one spraying Bolan's cheek with a dead man's blood, before the Executioner answered with a short burst of his own. The 5.56 mm tumblers punched his target backward, spinning him as he fell.

Bolan took off running toward the house. He didn't try to contact Johnny, who would've heard the gunfire and act accordingly. They'd known the soft probe wouldn't last for long, and hadn't meant to clear the property without a clash. From this point on it was do-or-die, and the game could still go either way.

Bolan had covered another forty-odd yards toward the house when a flashlight beam found him, then lost him, then came sweeping back to track him through the darkness. He ducked a split second before the first gunshot sounded, a slug chipping bark from the oak where he'd dropped his first kill.

Bolan returned fire on the run, without aiming, his CAR-15 spitting quiet 3- and 4-round bursts toward the shadows where muzzle-flashes winked and flared. The flashlight dropped immediately, spilling yellow light into the ferns as its owner devoted his full attention and both hands to self-defense.

How many guns?

There was no time to count them, but Bolan picked out the sounds of at least one pistol and a semiauto rifle as he ducked from tree to tree, running zigzag patterns through the night. The sudden echo of a shotgun blast behind him was more threatening, its spray of pellets more likely to bring down a moving target than all of the other weapons combined.

Bolan slid into cover behind a stout elm, letting several bullets sting the tree before he rolled out to his right, and scanned the night for muzzle-flashes.

Two weapons spoke at once, and Bolan tried for both shooters, milking short bursts from the CAR-15 at a range of something less than fifty feet. He scored on one of them, at least, heard the strangled cry of shock and pain as the gunner went down. The other ceased firing as well, though Bolan couldn't tell if he was hit or simply on the move.

The shotgunner took his cue from Bolan, firing at the carbine's muzzle-flash, but Bolan was already rolling away, behind the elm and out the other side. He was lined up and waiting when his adversary fired a second round, and that was all he needed to stitch the darkness with sizzling rounds.

Bolan waited a moment, deliberately exposed, to see if the shotgunner would try again. When he didn't, and another moment passed with no more sound except the call of worried voices from the mansion, he rose and left the killing ground behind.

More targets waited for him in the house, and Bolan didn't plan to keep them waiting long.

TODD GRIFFIN HAD ordered his team into action at the first sound of gunfire. Already on the cordless link to Garrett Tripp discussing threat assessments when the neighborhood power went down, he hadn't waited for orders when the shooting started. He was there to engage the enemy, and now he had his chance.

The team was small, but they were among the best available: two former Navy SEALs, two ex-Green Berets, one SAS veteran and a Spetznaz survivor from the one-time Soviet Bloc. Griffin wouldn't have bet against them if they were facing a regular battalion in the field, but he used a bit more caution this night, with the enemy still unknown.

He'd promised a callback and broken the link-up to Tripp, scrambling his troops at the same instant with a programmed signal on their two-way radios. Griffin was a second or two behind the other five but it made no real difference, since he was the fastest and fiercest of the lot.

They used insulated grappling hooks on the razor wire, not that the rubber sheathing was needed with lights out inside the compound. Unlike his faceless adversaries, Griffin knew that Joey DeMitri had no generators standing by in the event of an emergency. When the power went down, his so-called soldiers were blind—unlike Griffin's, with their night-vision goggles to scope out the lay of the land.

They'd missed one thing, though, and it was a big one. His spotters had reported no one entering the DeMitri estate before the shooting started. Dismissing the notion of negligence where these mercs were concerned, that meant either the enemy was that good, or he'd been inside already when they took their posts, waiting for the right time to strike.

Either way, it was hell on a Ferris wheel now, with guns blasting all over the place. Some of DeMitri's fat-cat neighbors were probably calling the police at that moment, and response time in a wealthy neighborhood like this one would be prompt.

Griffin had been told to do a job and to let no one interfere. Suppression of the enemy was paramount; it took priority over protocol and the usual rules about shunning contact with law-enforcement agencies. Whoever stood between Todd Griffin and his targets would be removed without hesitation or remorse.

Moving toward the big house and the sounds of battle,

Griffin almost hoped that some of DeMitri's goombahs would get in the way, or that some snot-nosed Metro Dade rookie would try to prevent them from leaving the scene. His blood was up, and he wouldn't rest easy until someone else's blood was spilled.

"Sound off at first sight of a target," he ordered his men, trusting the microphone to transmit his command. He expected no response and got none from the team. Orders were for obeying, not debating.

Griffin had barely broken a sweat as he neared the house, despite his camouflage fatigues, web gear, flack jacket, bandoliers, and the Steyr AUG assault rifle he carried. It was all in a night's work, more sport than hard labor.

Ninety seconds into the squeal, Griffin spotted his target—one of them, at least, moving toward the house. The soldier was dressed in black and painted to match, well armed and at ease on the field.

Griffin could've made the killing shot from where he stood, but he needed to know if there were more of the bastards around.

"I have one target, southwest side," he told the night. "Report contacts."

Four of the answers came back negative before the Russian hissed into his mick, "I have one, also. Northeast side. Engaging target."

"No!" Griffin commanded. "All troops respond to the locations noted. Clarify your marks before you move."

No way you get first blood, Ivan, he thought.

Smiling, Griffin set off in pursuit of his prey.

JOHNNY HAD NEARLY reached the house when he came under fire. He'd been prepared for contact ever since the shooting started on the other side of the estate, but the first rounds still surprised him, since they came from behind.

Dumb luck or providence saved him from the first short burst of automatic fire. Johnny was edging his way around a forked oak tree, ducking to avoid the gaze of a young sentry on patrol, when bullets slapped against the bark beside him, stinging him with slivers.

With no choice left to him, he slid around the oak, to put it at his back. The sentry saw him coming, raised a weapon to bring him under fire, then dropped to the grass as Johnny hit him with a short burst from his MP-5.

One down. How many more to go?

He turned his back to the house, feeling the exposure there, and risked a look through the deep notch in the forked tree that sheltered him. Shadows moved, advancing in a crouch. He counted three and sighted on the nearest of them from a range of thirty yards. Johnny was tightening his finger on the SMG's trigger when his target seemed to feel his danger and reacted on pure instinct.

They fired simultaneously, Johnny's target veering to the left and throwing himself to the ground. The others opened up a heartbeat later. Both weapons were suppressor-equipped, their muzzle-flashes tiny winking exclamation points of death.

Johnny swept the field with a burst from his SMG. Both runners went down, but he thought one of them fell with less grace than the other, more of a tumbling sprawl than a dive for cover. When the next spray of hostile fire came, he rolled out to the right, counting muzzle flares.

Only two.

Was the third gunner wounded or dead? And who were they? Stealth warriors imported to beef up DeMitri's security force? Or someone else?

Johnny fired at the muzzle-flashes, emptying his weapon's magazine, and fed the SMG a new one by touch, discarding the old. His gloves would leave no fingerprints, and every item of gear had been wiped clean at the safehouse, before they rolled out on their mission.

"I've got opposition here," he told Bolan through the headset's microphone. "Not Mob-style. More professional."

"Affirmative," his brother's voice came back. "Feels like a trap to me."

"Ideas?" Johnny asked, leaning out again to check for targets on the move.

"Screw it," Bolan replied. "Withdraw."

"Roger."

But saying it was one thing; actually pulling out was something else entirely. Now that they were in the trap, they couldn't simply walk away.

Not without spilling blood.

To emphasize the point, a pair of Joey DeMitri's watchdogs came at Johnny from the house, jogging across the lawn. One held a flashlight, probing for the source of muffled gunfire, while an Ingram MAC-10 machine pistol filled his other hand. The second had an M-16.

Johnny didn't wait for the bouncing beam of light to find him. He took the shooters down with a waist-high burst of autofire at fifty feet. They fell together in a twitching heap.

He felt the other hunters up and moving, even as the Mafiosi fell. Turning to bring them under fire, Johnny unloaded half his magazine at flitting shadows, hoping for a lucky hit. He was up and running by the time they started to return fire, no longer headed for the house, but back into the trees along a different path.

Withdraw. The order echoed in his ears.

If only he could make it to the wall alive.

VINCENT RUGGERO TRAILED behind his host and two gorillas bearing flashlights, three more shooters bringing up the rear.

He clutched a Colt .45 automatic in his right hand, drawing comfort from its solid weight. But from the racket outside Ruggero knew a pistol wouldn't do much good against the unknown enemy.

Who were these sons of bitches, trailing him halfway across the country? Why had they chosen this time to attack? How had they tracked him from Louisiana to Miami?

A leak in the Family.

Nothing else made any sense, but there was no way to pursue it at the moment. Before Ruggero could clean his own house, he had to get out of DeMitri's house alive.

"You say the limo's waiting?" he demanded.

"Standing by," DeMitri answered. "Don't give it another thought."

"Easy to say," Ruggero groused. "That isn't fireworks on the yard. It's not some kinda celebration in our honor. Get it?"

"Right," DeMitri snapped. "It's my boys cleaning house, is what it is. And since the cops'll be here any minute, we're retiring to a club I own in Broward County—where we spent the evening, by the way, with plenty of witnesses to say so if the DA wants to argue."

"Yeah," Ruggero muttered. "If we get there in one piece."

They passed through the dining room, kitchen and pantry, to reach a door at the rear of the house. One of the shooters opened it, peering out, and the sounds of gunfire were instantly louder, reverberating in the utility room where they stood.

"Where's the car?" Ruggero asked.

Before DeMitri could reply, headlight beams swept the doorway, making Ruggero wince and narrow his eyes. Instinct told him they were drawing too damned much attention, but all he wanted at the moment was a ride away from DeMitri's not-so-safe house to someplace remote and truly secure.

They broke for the limo, shooters going out ahead of the Dons to cover their exit, headlights burning tunnels through the night. Ruggero made a quick dash and dive toward the car.

"Who the fuck is that?" one of the forward shooters asked. He pointed through the windshield, just in case the rest of them were vague on what he meant.

A tall man, all in black, was standing in their path. He held some kind of military-looking weapon across his chest.

"Who cares?" DeMitri said. "Run the fucker down and get us out of here!"

The limo started forward, gaining speed. Ruggero saw the black-clad apparition raise his weapon, turning sideways as he sighted down the barrel.

Bullets pocked the limo's windshield, tearing bloody fragments from the driver's skull. Ruggero felt the car start to swerve toward the house, and they were still taking hits as a dead foot bore down on the accelerator, hurling them toward the cliff of a wall that gleamed bone-white in the wounded limo's headlights.

KEELY ROSS WAS READY in the Lexus, engine running sweet and nearly silent as she watched the mirrors, waiting for Cooper and Grant to appear. The volume of fire from inside Joey DeMitri's estate had increased, and she didn't know if the good guys were kicking ass or getting creamed.

And so she waited, as she'd promised to.

Were those sirens in the distance? Probably. It stood to reason that the neighbors would've summoned help by now.

If the cops showed up before her passengers arrived, what should she do? Running out on them didn't feel like an option, but she'd do them no good in custody, either. She could try to badge her way through any questions, but the blue suits might not be in a mood to respect federal credentials, much less swallow a story that was obviously full of holes.

Fight her way clear?

No good. Even if Ross possessed the temperament for a shootout with police, it would be tantamount to suicide. No good in that for herself or the others.

"Come on, goddammit!"

A shadow rolled across the top of DeMitri's fence and dropped to a crouch on the sidewalk. Seconds later, another man-shape touched down a few yards behind the first, the two of them looking like statues before they rose and started running toward the Lexus.

Ross palmed her Glock, index finger curling lightly around its trigger to release the built-in safety. She turned in her seat, extending her gun hand. Not aiming, exactly, but ready to fire through the open windows on the passenger's side. A bit more pressure on the trigger, and—

"You don't need that," Bolan told her, as he climbed into the back seat.

Johnny piled in behind him and slammed the door, snapping, "Hit it!"

Before she turned back, Ross saw a third shape tumble over the wall. This one crouched and aimed a weapon from the shoulder, silent flashes blinking from the muzzle. A bullet clanged against the Lexus.

She gunned it, peeling out from the curb as the rear window imploded and something cracked the windshield to her right. Cooper and Grant were returning fire now, and she caught a quick glimpse in the rearview as their target wobbled, toppling over backward in a sprawl.

They'd have to ditch the car, of course, but that was fine. As long as they were all—

"Dammit!"

Grant's curse brought her eyes back to the rearview mirror, where a pair of headlights bored through the night, close on their trail. Another long block took them out of the dark zone, back into the world where streetlights and porch lights held shadows at bay. For one fleeting moment Ross harbored a childish hope that their enemies would be trapped in the darkness, like vampires unable to face sunlight, but of course that was nonsense.

The chase car came after them, steadily closing the gap. Behind it, flashing lights showed her six or seven patrol cars converging on DeMitri's estate, their occupants seemingly oblivious to the pursuit in progress nearby.

Thank God for small favors, she thought, and bore down on the gas pedal.

"Left turn!" she warned her back seat passengers, taking the corner with a squeal of tortured rubber. The chase car followed, one of its passengers risking a shot once the squad cars had dropped out of sight. Ross heard something shatter.

"Somebody better get them off our ass while there's still time," she said.

Bolan lined up his shot through the vacant rear window, holding steady with the CAR-15 despite the swerving of the car.

He'd seen no more of the chase car than its headlights, but the space between them and their elevation from the pavement told him something of the vehicle's size. Not a sports car or compact, not a hulking SUV, but something in between.

Muzzle-blasts flared from both sides of the chase car, and Ross jerked her wheel in response. "Right turn!" she snapped, and took them through it on what felt like two wheels.

"Jumping Jesus!" Johnny yelled, then fired another burst from his MP-5 across the sedan's trunk. Bolan couldn't tell if the shots scored or not, but their enemies kept coming. Implacable. Relentless.

He flinched involuntarily as a bullet struck the trunk and ricocheted, gone somewhere in the night. Bolan found his mark and held it, aiming for a point three feet or so above the chase car's grille. Even if he was off by a matter of inches, grazing fire should accomplish his goal.

Unless one of the shooters dropped him first, or put a tracer through their fuel tank and turned the car into a rolling funeral pyre.

He stroked the carbine's trigger three times, holding steady on the mark as each burst of four or five rounds sped down range toward the onrushing target. One of the chase car's shooters was returning fire when the vehicle swerved radically, running through an S-curve in the middle of the two-lane residential street. It ended when the chase car jumped a curb and roared across a smallish lawn to collide with a parked Lincoln Town Car in the driveway. The Lincoln's alarm started whooping, silenced seconds later when its fuel tank exploded into flames.

"That's a wrap," Johnny said.

"Not quite," Ross corrected him. "This ride looks like something from Bonnie and Clyde. We'll need to ditch it pretty soon, or start attracting all the wrong kinds of attention."

"Can we get new wheels?" Johnny asked.

"Shouldn't be a problem," Ross answered, "one way or another."

"Let's do it," Bolan said, "we still have work to do, and it can't wait much longer."

**9**

*Miami*

The landline to Washington was crystal clear, thus allowing Bolan to pick up the uneasy tone in Hal Brognola's voice with no difficulty at all. He stood with rough brick to his back, pay phone in hand, watching traffic slide past him on Miami's Calle Ocho.

"You had quite a night," Brognola remarked.

"It was close."

"Heard the score yet?"

"There's nothing definite on the air down here, so far," Bolan replied.

"Well, they've got late returns at the Bureau. The OC boys are scrambling around the Hoover Building like their fannies are on fire."

"OC," the federal acronym for organized crime, had expanded since the 1980s to include a wide range of foreign and homegrown syndicates completely unrelated to the "traditional" Mafia.

"So, what's the word?" Bolan asked.

"Two birds with one stone, more or less," Brognola said.

"Joey DeMitri's dead and Vinnie Ruggero's on life support, waiting for his family to fly in from New Orleans and make a decision on treatment. Off the record, his EEG's flat-lined. He's not coming back."

"Two down," Bolan said.

In fact, he felt nothing for DeMitri or Ruggero aside from the sense of a mission accomplished. As for their next of kin, while he was willing to acknowledge their emotions at the loss of a husband, father or sibling, he was fresh out of sympathy. The two Families had prospered from human misery for generations—more than a century in Ruggero's case—and Bolan had no reason to believe they were about to change their ways. He hadn't stopped them, merely slowed them down a bit, but if it caused one or two of the new breed to reconsider a career in crime, so much the better.

But Bolan wouldn't hold his breath.

"We had some surprise opposition last night," he continued.

"Professional?" Brognola asked.

"Paramilitary," Bolan said.

"You're thinking the same crowd from Bayou LaFourche?"

"It had that feel. We dropped some of them, if you have a chance to check it out."

"Okay," Brognola said, "but don't get hopeful. The word from Metro-Dade is that all the dead around DeMitri's place were LCN.

La Cosa Nostra.

"No mercs in the body count, then?" he inquired.

"Not a one."

He tried another angle. "There was a pursuit," he told Brognola. "We took a carload of them off the road, a few miles south of DeMitri's place."

"Metro-Dade has the car," Brognola informed him, "with blood on the seats and the front passenger door, but no bodies inside or nearby. You know what that means."

The mercs were hiding their dead.

No man left behind, was the unwritten code of elite commando units everywhere, a point of honor insuring that no comrade, living or dead, would be left in enemy hands. In concrete terms it meant that his enemies had the numbers, the organization and presence of mind to retrieve their dead and wounded in the heat of urban combat, with sirens screaming in their ears.

It meant they weren't broken yet. Not by a long shot.

"I need anything you can tell me about Wayland Spade, his connections and background, whatever. I need it yesterday."

"It's in the pipe," Brognola said. "Meanwhile, you may want to give it a rest and let someone else pick up the pieces."

"No time for a handoff yet," Bolan said, "but I'd rather not be flying blind."

"They're pulling overtime at the Farm," the big Fed assured him. "Spade keeps a low profile, and then some."

Which simply meant he was professional. Bolan knew that already, despite the lapse with Keely Ross. It made the target more difficult to access and eliminate.

"How much time do you need?" Bolan asked.

Brognola considered the question. "A couple of hours, at least. Call it noon?"

"Noon it is."

He cradled the pay phone's receiver and walked back to the luxury sedan that had replaced the bullet-riddled Lexus. Come hell or high water, the Executioner would be riding in style.

All the way to the end of the line.

*Washington, D.C.*

AVERY KOONTZ WAS a bureaucratic survivor. First and foremost, he was adept at spotting political land mines and side-stepping before they blew up in his face. He had outlasted three administrations so far, and he had every intention of clinging to office when the present regime passed into history.

That's what survivorship was all about.

Koontz was conservative by disposition, but he wasn't a crusader. He didn't go looking for fights as a rule, considering his own longevity more critical than most attempts to revise public policy. He cherished a vision of the ideal society, granted, but he'd also spent enough time in politics and at the seat of U.S. government to realize that dreams seldom came true.

His posting to the Office of Homeland Security had been a distressing fluke. Koontz had no law-enforcement background. He had been drafted, more or less, from a midranking post at the Treasury Department, where he had spent three years despite a long-standing arithmetical deficit that prevented Koontz from balancing his own checkbook. Homeland Security was the hot new posting. It looked great on a résumé, and what the hell. If he could make it there, he could make it anywhere.

A true survivor, all the way.

But long-term survival in the District meant caution, above all else, and that was why Avery Koontz had been dreading the call that awaited him now, on line two. A part of him had hoped it would all go away, like a bad dream blown to tatters by the sound of an alarm clock, but that was not to be.

Koontz picked up the phone, forcing a smile despite the fact that there was no one in the office to see him. "Agent Ross," he said. "What's happening?"

And having asked the fateful question, he was forced to hear the answer. She told him what was happening, in terms he couldn't fudge, finagle or pretend he hadn't heard. She was spelling it out for him, chapter and verse, leaving Koontz in no doubt whatsoever that his career—and perhaps his very liberty—might be hanging by a thread.

Koontz listened to her story, not quite patiently but smart enough to avoid interrupting the flow. He didn't take notes, since conversations on his private line were automatically captured verbatim by a tape recorder hidden in the left-hand bottom drawer of his stylish desk. On a busy day he might use half a dozen two-hour tape cassettes, some of which he preserved as a matter of history or pure self-defense. This day's tape would remain unlabeled, locked away in his office safe.

Or perhaps he should simply burn it.

Ross finished her report and waited, giving Koontz a chance to speak. The line felt dread-heavy, as if she expected some kind of screaming tirade. Had they known each other longer than a few short months, she would've known that rants were not his style. In fact, Koontz made a practice of concealing agitation, anger and other unproductive emotions behind a facade of ineffable calm.

And he was very calm now, as he said, "So, these people are basically killing whoever they want to, vigilante-style, with the government's blessing?"

"You checked them," she reminded him, thereby sealing the fate of this tape.

"I verified a federal connection," Koontz replied. "No one showed me an all-purpose hunting license."

Sounding exasperated now, she asked him, "So, what should I do? You want me to forget about it? I can tell them we're pulling out, but there's no way I can bring them in without a King Kong SWAT team for backup. Even then, I wouldn't give you odds."

Koontz was stuck on the phrase we're pulling out, making it clear to anyone who heard the tape five minutes or five years from now that the Office of Homeland Security had been in on a plot that included mass murder and sundry lesser violations of state and federal law, piled up on each other to insure a minimum sentence of life without parole for all concerned.

The tape would definitely have to go.

With that in mind, he told Ross, "Don't be hasty. You reckon these wild men are getting results?"

"Of a sort," she replied. "Long-term, I can't say. It's a wait-and-see thing."

"Then by all means," Koontz said, "wait and see."

ABOUT THE TIME Avery Koontz was setting match to plastic in the private bathroom of his ninth-floor office suite on Constitution Avenue, Hal Brognola answered his telephone roughly a half mile to the north and west.

The call was right on time.

"Tell me," Brognola said by way of greeting.

"I've got what there is," Aaron Kurtzman replied. "If anyone else can find more, I want him or her on the staff."

"Duly noted. Now spill it."

"Wayland Arthur Spade," Kurtzman said without further preamble. "Born July 5, 1968, in Richland, Georgia. His father was regular Army, a lifer. Spade joined the Marine Corps out of high school and served two four-year tours in a recon platoon. He saw action in Kuwait, Somalia and Haiti. Decorated with a Purple Heart and Silver Star for action during Desert Storm. A month into his third tour, he fell under suspicion of stealing and selling government property."

"Let me guess," Brognola interrupted. "Weapons?"

"That's affirmative. The way his file reads, Spade had an accomplice—a lance corporal named Irwin Taggart—who was on the verge of rolling over for the prosecution when he died in a barracks fire at Paris Island. Arson was confirmed, but the JAG investigators couldn't specify the torch. It closed the case on Spade, but the Corps doesn't take stuff like that lying down. They basically started harassing Spade with every crap detail imaginable, until he snapped and assaulted a superior officer. He served the maximum brig time and left with a bad-conduct discharge."

"To become a merc," Brognola said, not asking.

"Right. We have confirmed involvement on three continents before he hooked up with the Isla de Victoria operation. He's billed himself as an instructor and adviser on missions to Africa, Asia and Central America. He backed the losing side in Rwanda and got out just in time, one jump ahead of a war crimes indictment. Something about village massacres with Spade in charge. The details are fuzzy."

"And they have no extradition treaty," Brognola observed.

"Another saving grace for Mr. Spade," Kurtzman agreed. "From there, he came back to the States, then signed on with Maxwell Reed's Victorian Liberation Movement, helping the cause on Isla de Victoria—for a price, of course."

"Let me guess. Instructor and adviser?"

"What else?" Kurtzman paused, then said, "There's something else, though."

"What?" Brognola prodded him.

"Spade's not the man in charge."

Brognola blinked at that and asked, "Who is?"

"Another merc," Kurtzman replied. "One Garrett Wesley Tripp, born on Halloween 1966 in Boise, Idaho. He finished high school and got a year of community college before he joined the Navy. He aced SEAL training and served a four-year tour before discharge. He was involved in training Contra rebels for a while."

"What kind of discharge?" Brognola asked.

"Honorable. My guess is they would've kept him on forever, if he'd wanted to stay."

"What made him leave?"

"Unknown. After his separation, Tripp took another shot at college, but he couldn't make the grades. Looks like he reverted to what he does best and decided to turn a profit with it, instead of spending his life in line at the PX."

"What's he done that we know of?"

"The same pattern as Spade, but more so. Over the past dozen years, he's traceable to mercenary actions in fifteen countries, from Nicaragua to Sri Lanka. Tripp's been running his own show for a few years, offering a range of services from small-arms instruction to executive action. He met Spade roughly a year after setting up shop for himself, some kind of mercenary trade show in Las Vegas, and they've been together ever since. The deal with Maxwell Reed is their top job, so far. It could let them retire if they put him on top."

"So, who finances Reed?" Brognola asked.

"We're still working on that," Kurtzman said. "But based on his ties to Ruggero and DeMitri, I'm guessing it isn't the Dade County Chamber of Commerce."

"We need to know the people pushing this," Brognola said, stating the obvious. "We've got people exposed. They can't do their jobs without knowing the opposition."

"We're tracking paper corporations," Kurtzman said. "Just a little more time."

"We're running out," Brognola advised him. "Take whatever shortcuts you can."

"Roger that."

As he cradled the receiver, Brognola was already planning his next conversation. His turn to give the briefing, this time.

He only hoped it wouldn't be too little and too late.

*Hialeah, Florida*

THEY GATHERED at the bungalow, sitting around the table in its modest dining room. Bolan, fresh off the telephone with Brognola, was running down the latest information on their enemies. Johnny and Keely Ross listened, memorizing the details, interjecting questions or comments as they came to mind.

"They faked me out," Ross said. "I thought Spade was the man in charge."

"You weren't far wrong," Bolan conceded. "He's Tripp's number two, and he was running the Louisiana end himself."

"Which begs the question," Johnny said. "If we put them out of business on Bayou LaFourche, where's their alternate training facility?"

"Who says they have one?" Ross asked.

"Tripp and Spade are professionals," Bolan replied. "They'd have a backup facility ready to run, just in case. They might even be using it now, if they have enough trainees and don't like putting all their eggs in one basket."

"A second camp." Ross sounded glum. "In the United States?"

"Could be," Johnny answered. "With their syndicate connections, the real estate's no problem. Any place with conditions similar to their target would fit the bill."

"Then again," Ross replied, "they might figure one bust in the States sours the whole patch. If it was me, I'd want my backup camp beyond the reach of pesky Feds."

"Makes sense," Bolan admitted. "Do you have a place in mind?"

"Not really. I was thinking somewhere south of the border. Maybe way south, like Guatemala or Honduras."

"It would help," Johnny noted, "if we knew who's paying the bills. It's hard for me to picture Joey DeMitri and his pal Ruggero funding a revolution on their own."

Bolan had reached the same conclusion, but he didn't know who else the mobsters might have recruited.

"We're still missing pieces," he said. "Until we have more of the puzzle in place, we're just guessing."

"So, what's the next move?" Ross inquired.

"Are you sure you want to know?" Johnny asked her.

"Hey, I told you I'm on board. It's cleared at the top."

Bolan wasn't so sure about that. Stony Man and its agents were granted a freedom of movement enjoyed by few—if any—other federal agencies. Government officers were bound by rules of procedure that made their jobs more difficult, and sometimes virtually impossible. Some chose to bend or effectively ignore those rules, but they were the exception, and none to Bolan's knowledge had abandoned the standard program of evidence collection and prosecution so completely that they mimicked Stony Man's more direct approach to crime fighting.

Hal Brognola's team was the court of last resort, the handlers of dirty work no other department or agency would touch for fear of scandal and/or ruin. As such, Bolan and his handful of comrades stood in a covert class by themselves.

Had Keely Ross truly been cleared by her superiors to participate in a Stony Man campaign? And if not, what were the obvious alternatives? Was she being dangled as bait, in some scheme to subvert Brognola's team? If so, by whom?

Or was she simply being cast adrift by someone at Homeland Security, to see what happened next?

The latter option offered maximum deniability for her supervisors, while leaving Ross totally exposed. It sounded like something the Feds would attempt, and while Bolan was willing to accept Ross's help, he didn't plan on letting her get in his way.

He felt the redhead watching him, her bright eyes scanning his face, seeking evidence of doubt. "You don't believe me?" she challenged.

"In my experience," he answered, "most bureaucrats play by the rules. They'd rather fail than be accused of showing some initiative."

"Not necessarily."

"So," Johnny said, "you're telling us you got no static for last night?"

"They weren't happy about it," Ross said, "but you checked through the system. I've got a provisional clearance."

"Meaning what?" Johnny asked her.

"Meaning we're good to go, for now," she said.

"And if they have a change of heart?"

"I'll take my chances."

Maximum deniability, Bolan repeated to himself. He wondered if the lady's boss would hang her out to dry when things got tough.

Make that tougher.

"That good enough for you?" he asked.

"I'm in," she said. "Let's hear the plan."

He paused for one more beat, considering the risk. "All right. Here's what we'll do."

KEELY ROSS THOUGHT the plan was outrageous, verging on crazy, but that didn't mean it would fail. On the contrary, in fact. As she watched and listened to Cooper running it down, and Grant tweaking details and adding suggestions of his own, she managed to convince herself that it could work.

Assuming they weren't all killed in the first few seconds, that was.

The two men would've relegated her to a driver's role again, but Ross wouldn't sit still for that. She demanded a more active part in the plan, and they finally agreed, albeit with clear reservations.

She didn't think their doubts sprang from a question of ability. She had already proved her competency in a crisis, whether it was driving hot wheels at top speed or fighting toe-to-toe, shot-for-shot with heavies who wanted her dead. Ross didn't count the fact that she'd been taken hostage, since that had occurred before she met Grant and Cooper. Once she was out of the lockup and had both feet on the ground, she'd acquitted herself on par with most men she could name.

Not these two, perhaps, but most men.

The battle in the swamp had been encouraging. She'd done her part, covered the flanks as well as anybody else—but they'd still demoted her to driving on the second hit.

She understood that. Grant and Cooper obviously knew each other from way back, sharing a wealth of experience Ross could never hope to tap. It was almost as if they were kin of some kind, though she had looked in vain for a physical resemblance. Beyond the dark hair and athletic physiques they were nothing alike—until you spoke to them or watched them work. The similarity was nothing tangible, but it made them one hell of a team.

And it left Keely Ross on the outside, looking in.

Another problem, clearly, was her status with the Office of Homeland Security. Ross wasn't sure exactly what agency Grant and Cooper represented, though Koontz had checked it out in Washington and pronounced it legit without filling in any significant details. A week ago, Ross wouldn't have believed the U.S. government had any group detailed to stage domestic vigilante raids and gun down suspects without any semblance of legal procedure. It would have shocked her to the core last week, before she'd been abducted by savages, threatened with torture and death.

This day, somehow, the concept didn't sound so bad.

The problem, Ross thought, was that Grant and Cooper had trouble accepting even a partial conversion on her part. Despite all that had passed between them in the past two days, they still expected her to quail in the face of danger, or perhaps to run off and report them for stepping over the line. Therefore, they tried to keep her sidelined, on the periphery of the action, where she was comparatively safe and simultaneously rendered useless as a witness.

Not this time.

The plan might blow up in their faces, but she'd been there when the fuse burned down, no matter what. If there was hell to pay at the end of the line, Keely Ross meant to pick up her share of the tab.

Even if she had to pay in blood.

**10**

*Miami*

Time zones were the second-worst part of spreading bad news
on a global scale. The true worst, as Garrett Tripp knew from
experience, was breaking bad news to a group of unpredict-
able, potentially homicidal investors. Every time he dialed the
telephone, Tripp knew he might be setting off a chain reaction that could blow up in his face and drop him in a shallow
grave.

He didn't really think the investors would try to kill him,
either individually or jointly, but he could never be sure. They
were men long accustomed to having things their own way,
punishing those who opposed them and removing obstacles
by brute force.

All things considered, Tripp would have preferred to del-
egate the task to a subordinate, but he believed that men who
had invested millions in a project were entitled to the truth,
and they deserved to hear it from the individual in charge.

And there was no one Tripp trusted more with the potentially deadly chore than he trusted himself.

Spade wasn't a candidate, after last night. He'd nearly

bought the farm himself, chasing the raiders after they fled from DeMitri's estate. Spade swore there were no more than two or three shooters involved, but Tripp took that opinion with a hefty grain of salt. Spade had barely managed to remove his dead and wounded from the scene before police arrived, and he wouldn't have managed that without a couple of quick-thinking subordinates on-site at DeMitri's home.

They still had zero official exposure, nothing in the media at all, but Tripp knew that could change the next time someone sprang a trap. So far, reporters in two states had been content to speculate on rumbles in "The Underworld", whatever that might mean. The latest pipe dream was a war between Ruggero and DeMitri, though it failed to explain why both Dons were riding in the same car when they went down. Theories of an alleged kidnapping generally named Ruggero as the victim, but one imaginative tabloid hack claimed both Mafiosi were snatched by an unknown rival, then shot by mistake when their own men botched a rescue.

Tripp wasn't concerned with public perceptions of recent events, as long as his name and the names of his people weren't mentioned. His employers were infinitely more dangerous than any police force, hamstrung as law-enforcement agents were with petty rules and procedures. His employers made excellent friends and perilous enemies. If they set their minds to it, any one of the investors could probably make Tripp disappear in the time it took authorities to secure a search warrant.

Unless he saw them coming, of course.

Tripp had planned out the series of calls for convenience, noting the various time zones in advance, charting a course of sorts as if he were about to circle the globe in a rocket, instead of simply reaching out from his cheap storefront office with long-distance calls. He would be using a standard phone scrambler for security's sake, as he always did when consultation with the various investors was required. It wasn't an issue of hiding, since any one of the principals could find him at will, but at least eavesdroppers would be frustrated.

Grim-faced, he reached out for the telephone.

*Messina, Sicily*

DANTE AMBROSIO TOOK the call at 5:13 p.m., roused from a midday nap that had featured a dream of his favorite niece. In dreams, Ambrosio showed her a side of himself that would have startled his brother Giancarlo, had Giancarlo still been alive.

It was too bad about Giancarlo, Ambrosio thought, but he never should have sided with the Corsicans against his own flesh and blood. For such *infamia* his execution had been mandatory. Giancarlo's treachery had left his only daughter defenseless in a world of predators.

Don Ambrosio was smiling when the houseman shook him gently awake. The servant wore a worried expression, clearly afraid that the interruption might result in punishment. Ambrosio was dwelling on the possibilities when he heard the name of his caller and trivia vanished from his mind.

"Bring me the telephone at once," he ordered, sitting upright on the sofa where he'd drifted off to sleep.

The houseman produced a cordless phone and handed it to Don Ambrosio, then retreated from the room in waddling haste. Ambrosio called after him to switch on the scrambler.

"Yes, sir," the houseman said across his shoulder. "It's already done."

Ambrosio let the door close before he lifted the telephone to his ear and spoke into the mouthpiece. "Mr. Tripp," he said. "Always a pleasure."

"Not this time, sir, I'm afraid," Tripp replied.

"More bad news?" Ambrosio's tone was mild. He didn't have to shout for this man to recognize his mood.

"Yes, sir. There was an incident at Don DeMitri's home, here in Miami. He's been killed, sir. Don Ruggero was also gravely injured."

"Will he live?" Ambrosio asked.

"Perhaps, with the assistance of machines."

"A pity. And the rest?"

The question sounded casual. In fact, Ambrosio was more concerned with the fate of their mission than with the health of his long-distance comrades. DeMitri and Ruggero were weaklings in Ambrosio's view, their proud Sicilian blood diluted by life in America. He wouldn't miss them personally, but it would be grim news if their passing derailed the project.

In that case, Ambrosio decided, heads would roll.

"We're still on track," Tripp reassured him. "We've had some loss of personnel, but nothing I can't handle."

"Are you handling it, in fact?"

"Yes, sir."

"I take it, then, that you've identified the men responsible?"

"We're working on it, sir."

"The answer would be 'no,' then."

"For the moment, that's correct," Tripp granted.

"For the moment," Ambrosio echoed. "You expect progress, then?"

"At the moment, sir, the situation's well in hand. Consider this a courtesy call, to keep you informed."

"I consider it a duty," Ambrosio replied. He let a hint of steel enter his tone. "The seven million dollars I've invested is worth more than simple courtesy, I think."

"Of course," Tripp said. "I didn't mean—"

"To insult me? Of course not. I take that for granted."

"Thank you, sir."

"Thank me by resolving this problem, Mr. Tripp. You came recommended as a security expert. I hope that was no exaggeration."

"No, sir. You have my word on that."

"I prefer deeds, Mr. Tripp. You take my meaning?"

"Indeed I do, sir."

"Very good. In that case, I'll be watching your progress and looking forward to a prompt solution. One way or another."

Tripp didn't have to ask what Ambrosio meant by that comment. He signed off as quickly as possible, adding one more apology for the inconvenience of his call. Ambrosio excused him and set the cordless phone on the nearby coffee table.

More trouble in America, and Tripp was holding out on him. There'd been no mention of the killings in Louisiana, but Ambrosio knew about them all the same. He had eyes inside Vincent Ruggero's Family, and in Joey DeMitri's, as well.

Tripp had tried to deceive him, minimizing the damage they had suffered thus far. It was understandable, from the viewpoint of self-preservation, and Ambrosio would not penalize the man for trying to save face—as long as he cleared up the problem without delay. If there were further losses, though, or any other efforts to mislead the primary investors Ambrosio might have to undertake a change in personnel.

And those who thought him weak, perhaps too far removed from the United States to take an active role in the festivities, would face a rude surprise.

*St. Petersburg, Russia*

SEMYON BORODIN WAS sipping peach-flavored vodka, enjoy-ing the presence of two naked women seated on either side of him, when his cell phone chirped shrilly at 7:48 p.m. Bo-rodin frowned at Nicolai Yurochka, seated across the low table and sandwiched between two more women.

Who would be calling him here, at the club where he came to relax?

"Da?"

"Mr. Borodin," the caller said in English. "I'm sorry for the interruption, sir."

Borodin recognized the voice at once. He had a facility for voices, also names and faces. He remembered friends and foes alike, although the latter seldom lived long enough to register beyond a first impression.

"Always a pleasure," Borodin said. He lied as a matter of courtesy. Pleasure, he wagered, had little or nothing to do with Tripp's call. "How can we help each other this fine day?"

Tripp told him what had happened overnight—or some of it, at least—while Borodin sat listening and clutched his telephone with fingers blanched by rage. He heard the mer-cenary out, silently complimenting himself on the fact that he wasn't yet raving obscenities or smashing the phone in fury. It took self-control to refrain from such outbursts in public.

"It sounds serious," Borodin said when Tripp was fin-ished.

"It could be worse, sir," Tripp assured him. "These things happen."

"I believe you're paid quite handsomely to stop them from happening. Is that not so?"

"Spilt milk, sir," Tripp said. "We're taking remedial measures to make sure there's no repetition of last night's events."

Borodin knew it was time to drop the other shoe. "But Mr. Tripp," he said, "it's not the first time, is it?"

"Sir?" Feigning confusion, while he stalled for time.

"Two nights before your latest mishap, I believe there was another difficulty in New Orleans, yes? You failed to mention it, but bad news has a way of traveling."

"It wasn't in New Orleans, sir. It was—"

"I don't need lessons in geography!" Borodin snapped. "Right now, you need to tell me why I'm better off with you alive, rather than dead and buried."

"The investors chose me for my record and my expertise," Tripp answered. Borodin was grudgingly impressed by his steady voice, but that would swiftly change if the six thousand miles between them should evaporate and Borodin could reach the mercenary's throat.

"Your record is impressive, but it's ancient history. We need results now."

"You'll have them, sir. I promise you."

"I hope so, Mr. Tripp. Nine million dollars may be petty cash, but if I think you've lost it for me, there'll be no place in the world for you to hide. I hope we understand each other."

"Yes, sir. Perfectly."

"Then do your job."

Borodin broke the link and placed his cell phone on the table, picking up his vodka glass before he settled back against the sofa. On his left, the brunette leaned in close and whispered something nasty in his ear.

"That sounds like fun," Borodin said. "Let's do it twice."

*Tokyo*

KENJI TANAKA WAS weighing matters of life and death when his chief of security entered the chamber at 3:12 a.m. Kneeling before him on a mat of woven straw, one of his minor subordinates had been reduced to blubbering tears by the prospect of looming oblivion.

The penitent, Hideki Ito, barely noticed the appearance of a new arrival in the room. He had already pled his case, such as it was, first claiming that he didn't know how forty-seven thousand yen had vanished from the betting parlor he managed on Tanaka's behalf, then breaking down to admit that he had embezzled the money to finance rehabilitation for a drug-addicted relative. Tanaka, in fact, already knew that Ito spent most of the money on his sixteen-year-old mistress, tucked away in Maebashi where Ito thought no one could find her.

She'd been found, of course, and the rest was history. Tanaka had her waiting, gagged and trussed for slaughter, in a room just down the hall. He hadn't shown the girl to Ito yet, because he wanted to see if the man could speak truthfully in defense of his own worthless life. Now that vital question had been answered, but Tanaka's judgment was delayed by the arrival of his agent, bowing deeply to apologize as he held out a tiny cell phone, pleading with Tanaka to accept an urgent call from the United States.

Barbarians. They never thought about the hour or the international date line.

Tanaka accepted the instrument, stone-faced. His breeding forbade him from snapping at the inconsiderate caller, but he made no attempt to be gracious.

"Good morning, Mr. Tripp."

"Sir, I apologize for the intrusion at this hour. I have news that really shouldn't wait."

"By all means, then, enlighten me."

The tale was simply told, deserving and receiving no embroidery. Tanaka listened stoically, his eyes never leaving Hideki Ito's tear-streaked face. If any anger showed on his face, Tanaka wanted the thief to see it aimed in his direction.

When Tripp finished speaking Tanaka asked him, "When will you be able to resolve the situation?"

"We're shooting for twenty-four hours maximum, sir."

Tanaka made no mention of his six million-dollar investment. Tripp would not have forgotten, and belaboring the point was undignified. Instead, he simply said, "So be it. Please keep me informed."

"Of course, sir."

Tanaka handed the cell phone back to his chief of security and watched the man bow himself out of the room, walking backward until he reached the door. Still without taking his eyes from Ito's reddened face, Tanaka told Tomichi Kano, "Bring the woman."

There were moments in the life of every Yakuza chief when he had to make critical decisions on the spur of the moment. Tanaka's investment with Garrett Tripp and Maxwell Reed had been made after due consideration, consultation with accountants and lawyers to help the boss make up his mind. Other decisions required immediate action, however, and solicitation of second opinions would be viewed as a sign of fatal weakness.

Hideki Ito's situation was a case in point.

So, one day soon, might be the case of Garrett Tripp.

*Cali, Colombia*

HECTOR SANTIAGO was midway through his fourteenth lap of the Olympic-sized swimming pool when he heard Pablo Aznar calling out his name. Aznar knew better than to interrupt his nightly swim, the breach of etiquette telling Santiago that he was about to confront a crisis. He stroked to the nearest ladder and hauled himself out of the water, accepting a towel from Aznar.

"What is it, Pablo?"

"The mercenary. Tripp. He's on line two from Miami."

"More trouble?"

"What else?" Aznar scowled. "I told you the gringo was worthless."

"He's fought many wars," Santiago reminded his aide.

"And I wonder how many he lost."

Santiago finished toweling his chest, arms and hands as he approached the wrought-iron table where a telephone awaited him. It had buttons for three different lines, the second one presently glowing bright orange. Santiago dropped his towel onto a desk chair, lifted the receiver and thumbed down the illuminated button.

"Tripp, what is it?"

"Sir, we've run into a bit of difficulty here."

"Explain."

He did, not rushing through the story, but reporting the crucial details in something under ninety seconds. Santiago respected economy, while at the same time suspecting Tripp of trying to minimize the damage. The Colombian had eight million reasons to worry about such deception by the man who was supposed to guarantee his investment's security. Still, it would not do to make the soldier suspicious, particularly if Santiago needed to remove him from his position by force.

"We have a bargain Mr. Tripp. Is that correct?"

"Of course, sir," Tripp replied.

"I trust you to resolve these matters in a timely fashion, without drawing any needless attention to me or the other investors."

"I understand, sir."

"Are you able to do that?" Santiago pressed him.

"Yes, sir. That's a guarantee."

"In which case, we should have no difficulty. Call me at once when the problem is resolved, sí?"

"Of course, sir."

Santiago hung up the phone and watched the lighted button go dark. He felt Aznar watching him and spoke without meeting his subordinate's gaze. "Reach out to Calderon and Benitez in Miami. Tell them to keep a close watch over Tripp from now on. Have them ready to move if I give the word to take him out."

"Perhaps I should go there myself," Aznar said. "If there's trouble, let me be your eyes."

Santiago turned to face Aznar then. The man was like a brother to him. They had come up together from nothing, fighting for their lives on the streets of Medellín, advancing from service as cut-rate assassins and mules to command the country's second-largest drug cartel. Within a year or eighteen months, Santiago believed that their major competitors would cease to exist, leaving himself and Aznar on top of the heap.

Unless he let the clumsy gringos drag him down.

"Be careful in Miami," he said at last. "It would be inconvenient to replace you just now."

*Panama City*

SUN ZU-WANG WAS relaxing in a steaming bath, head barely visible above the deep tub's marble lip, when the gold-plated telephone mounted on the wall above him emitted its soft purring sound. He glanced at his Rolex watch, resting on the toilet seat within arm's reach, and saw that it was nearly seven p.m.

The phone purred again and he shook one hand dry before reaching up for the receiver. The bathroom telephone received no calls directly from outside Sun's house. All incoming calls were screened by his staff. Only the most important passed through to disturb him when he found time for himself.

"What is it?" he demanded.

"Garrett Tripp from the United States, sir," one of the housemen answered. "He says it's vital that you speak to him immediately."

"Put him through," Sun told the houseman.

"Yes, sir."

Two muffled clicks were followed by the sound of Tripp's voice. "Hello? Mr. Sun?"

"I am here," Sun replied.

"Please accept my apology for the intrusion, sir."

"It's nothing."

"I'm afraid there's been some trouble here," Tripp said.

Sun listened to the tale of violence perpetrated by a band of unknown enemies. One of their investors was dead, another kept alive by pumps and electrodes. It was troubling, to say the least, though Sun felt nothing personally for the two Italians or their soldiers.

"What of my investment?" he asked Tripp, cutting to the heart of the matter.

"Sir, the funds have not been jeopardized. The operation is intact and proceeding on schedule."

"Who picks up the slack without DeMitri and Ruggero?" Sun inquired.

"When their replacements are selected, we assume the new leaders of their respective Families will continue with the program in good faith."

"And if they don't?"

"I'm confident that they can be persuaded to remain on board," Tripp said.

Sun knew what that meant. The new Mafia Dons would face war if they tried to back out of the bargain made by their late predecessors. Sun had no quarrel with such tactics, as long as he was not asked to participate without some form of compensation.

"And what of those responsible?" he asked. It was the second crucial question, possibly more vital than the first.

"We'll have them soon, sir. Trust me."

"Trust is perilous," Sun told the mercenary. "When it fails, a vacuum is created. Dreadful things transpire."

"I have no fear on that score, Mr. Sun," Tripp answered.

"No?" Perhaps you should, Sun thought. "In that case, please keep me informed."

"Of course, sir. While I have your ear, I'd like to ask a favor, if I may."

The man's audacity was startling. It almost made Sun smile.

"What favor?"

Tripp explained. It was unorthodox, but nothing difficult. Sun reckoned it would cost him nothing in the long run.

"Very well," he said. "See to it, then. Goodbye."

Sun reached above his head, eyes closed, and cradled the receiver by feel. He had nine million U.S. dollars invested in the operation so far, with nothing of substance to show for it, but he refused to worry yet. If worse came to worst, he would take every penny of it from Tripp's own flesh. It wasn't the ideal solution, granted, but the prospect was a pleasant one.

Smiling, Sun reached out for a bar of scented soap.

*Fort Lauderdale*

MAXWELL REED WAS DOZING when a rapping on his bedroom door pulled him back from the murky realm of sleep. The sounds of gunfire frightened Reed at first, until he realized that they were coming from the TV set and not the grounds outside.

One of the islanders, a hulking bodyguard named Merrill, stuck his head in the doorway and blinked at Reed. "You have a call from Mr. Tripp," he said.

Reed sighed. The telephone beside his bed was disconnected for a reason. He received calls day and night—from cranks, supporters, journalists, vindictive white supremacists, prospective fiancées—but they were screened by Reed's security staff. He spoke personally to no more than two or three percent of the callers, and to most of those simply as an act of common courtesy. Soon, if his mission was successful, he would be exempt even from that.

Garrett Tripp, however, could not be avoided. And that was sad, for of late he always seemed to bring bad news.

The television told him it was nearly eight o'clock.

Reed fumbled with the telephone cord behind his bed, sleepy fingers needing three attempts to find the wall jack. Finally he did it and then lifted the receiver to his ear.

"Good evening, Mr. Tripp. How may I help you?"

"I think you should get out of town for a while," Tripp replied.

"Excuse me?" Reed was wide-awake now, sitting upright in bed. He groped for the television's remote control and muted the canned sounds of battle.

"We're looking high and low for the men who iced De-Mitri and Ruggero," Tripp explained, "but it's taking longer than expected. In the meantime, I think you should find a safer place to spend some time. Until we clean this up, I mean."

"Safer? Where would I go?" The very thought confused

Reed. What was Tripp suggesting? Was it all some kind of trick?

"I was thinking Panama City," the mercenary replied. "Nice weather, no tropical storms at the moment, and one of our investors has his home base there."

"Sun Zu-Wang."

"That's correct, sir. I've taken the liberty of speaking with Mr. Sun this afternoon, and he's agreed to offer you his hospitality for the duration. That's if you're amenable, of course."

"When would I leave?" Reed asked.

"How soon can you get packed?"

"I've no idea. Perhaps an hour?"

"Perfect. I've got people on the way. You've made a wise decision, sir. Good night."

Reed lowered the receiver to its cradle, trying to make sense of thoughts that tumbled through his mind. Above all else, he wondered when he had become a chess piece, moved across a vast and empty board by someone else's hand.

## 11

*South Florida*

Bolan was running short of targets in Miami. He hadn't finished off his local enemies, by any means, but Joey DeMitri's men had gone to ground, and Bolan had no address for any of the mercenaries who had been employed to help with preparations for the Caribbean revolution. Without locations, he couldn't reach out and touch anyone.

Which brought him back to Maxwell Reed.

The self-styled president in exile was a sitting duck, killing time at his pad in Fort Lauderdale. Bolan wasn't convinced of Reed's leadership role in the plot—hell, he wasn't sure exactly what the plot itself entailed, so far—but he was willing to bet that Reed had answers at his disposal. Information that could tell the Executioner who and where his true enemies were.

The island diplomat's estate was under guard. No great surprise on that score, although the racial composition of the security team gave Bolan pause. He'd expected a crew of Reed's islanders, men like the ones he'd encountered at Bayou LaFourche, to be watching their president while he slept. And they were there—but not alone. Mingling with the dark faces were white ones, rugged soldier-types so similar in bearing that they could've been related, despite the fact that no two truly resembled one another.

Mercenaries.

They were out in force, patrolling Reed's estate side-by-side with a hardforce of island warriors who seemed to be carved from mahogany and teak. The guards on Reed's wrought-iron front gates weren't showing any hardware, but the troops inside his walled grounds were armed to the teeth with shotguns and assault rifles. Their weapons might be semiauto versions of the standard military models, to conform with state and federal firearms laws, but Bolan wasn't betting on it. Either way, it took only one hit to put a human target down and out for good.

Bolan counted sixteen shooters in the aerial photo, snapped hours earlier by a local charter pilot who couldn't say no to the four-figure price for a half hour's work. He calculated there would be a backup force of nearly equal size inside the house. Call it a possible forty guns, to be on the safe side. All that, plus a potential surprise in waiting from whatever mobile team Garrett Tripp and Waylon Spade might have to spare. If DeMitri's survivors were feeling a need for revenge, well, then that could get sticky, too.

"All ready?" Bolan asked his two companions.

Johnny nodded, bright eyes flashing in his blacked-out face.

"As ready as I'll ever be," said Keely Ross.

They'd done their final weapons and equipment checks. Standing in the darkness of a balmy night, a hundred yards from Reed's private fortress, they couldn't know when—or if—they would all be together again. There was a sense of parting and potential loss that Bolan felt each time he went to battle with a comrade, knowing it could be the last time they were face-to-face and living to enjoy it.

They'd charted their approach from the aerial photos. All they needed now was the signal to proceed. Bolan gave that signal at 3:19 a.m. and watched his brother move off through the shadows, with Ross trailing two steps behind. Bolan checked his watch, then counted off another sixty seconds in his head before he followed, watching for neighborhood patrols.

It was a risky proposition, tackling Reed and his defenders so soon after the blowout with DeMitri and Ruggero, but Bolan had no choice. They were fresh out of leads, and without new direction their campaign was stalled.

Tripp's figurehead had suddenly become the only game in town.

WAYLAND SPADE KNEW a last-ditch defense when he saw one, and the stakeout at Reed's place in Fort Lauderdale had all the earmarks. The only saving grace, so far, was that Joey DeMitri's heir apparent, one Danny Alessio, had turned up with twenty surplus shooters in response to a telephone call.

"Same deal as with the old man, right?" was all he asked.

Watching Reed's house felt like a spell of busywork, but in the current atmosphere of violence Spade couldn't be sure. They still had no fix on the raiders, beyond an appearance of limited numbers, and that only made it more embarrassing when the strangers kept kicking Spade's ass. His stock had plummeted with Tripp already. One more loss like last time, and...

He put the thought away and drained his coffee mug, leaving it near the sink in Reed's spacious kitchen before he went out to review the troops. Surprise inspections kept them on their toes, a goal more problematic with Reed's islanders than with his own seasoned mercs. Now that Alessio's men were tossed into the mix, Spade wasn't sure what to expect on his tour of the grounds.

Spade was at the kitchen door, one hand clamped around the knob and twisting it, when someone gave a shout from the grounds outside. He couldn't identify the voice, but there was no time to consider the problem in any case. The shout had barely registered with Spade's conscious mind before a shot rang out.

And then all hell broke loose.

It started with a kind of ripple effect, gunfire expanding from the point of the initial shot, spreading rapidly until it sounded as if the estate were surrounded, defenders battling with invaders on all sides. Spade couldn't begin to identify all the weapons in use.

What he did know, with ironclad certainty, was that he had to find out what in hell was happening. He had to know right now, goddammit, and he had to clean it up before the cops rolled up to interfere. If someone's itchy trigger finger had sparked the fireworks over nothing, Spade promised himself he'd be wearing it on a necklace by sunrise.

But if the phantom enemy was back...

Spade wore an H&K MP-5 K submachine pistol—the stubby two-handed room broom—in a shoulder rig beneath his left armpit. He cleared it now and whipped the cocking lever through its short cycle to chamber a 9 mm round. The weapon's fire-selector switch was set for 3-round bursts. If the SMG failed him, Spade had a SIG-Sauer P-229 semiauto pistol holstered at the small of his back, and his belt buckle was the square palm grip of a razor-edged dagger.

Come what may, Spade was ready to join in the games.

As if to reinforce that thought, as he stepped through the kitchen doorway into darkness, an explosion echoed from the grounds. Spade saw the flicker of its fiery blossom, off to his left in the trees, near the estate's southeastern perimeter. The ghost of a shock wave reached him seconds later, lightly brushing his cheeks.

It was as good a place to start as any.

The blast meant strangers on the property, since none of Spade's defenders had been issued hand grenades. And that, in turn, meant targets ready for the kill.

Spade had a chance to wrap it up right here, redeem himself and save the day.

Smiling, he gripped the MP-5 and plunged into the night.

IT WAS déjà vu all over again.

Johnny was trying for a soft probe, mindful of his brother's wish to question Maxwell Reed, but the play went sour with barely ninety seconds on the clock. A sentry who'd been crouching in the bushes, either playing smart or simply slacking off, sprang up in front of Johnny like a jack-in-the box. He could've fired from hiding, ending it right there, but something made him try to take the intruder alive.

"Hey!" he shouted, leveling a riot shotgun from the hip, left-handed.

Johnny fired without thinking about it, a quiet 3-round burst from his H&K submachine gun. It wasn't the cleanest of kills, but it took his man down. The shotgun lost its fix on Johnny, but it still discharged as the gunner collapsed, a spray of buckshot clipping leaves from the branches overhead.

Terrific.

The shotgun blast was instantly echoed by gunfire nearby, spreading rapidly around the estate's walled perimeter. Johnny assumed that Reed's islanders were responsible for most of the shooting, taking it for granted that Spade's mercenaries would have more self-control. Whatever the source, though, none of the rounds had come close to him so far, and Johnny pressed on toward the house, covering ground while he could, before someone else showed up to oppose him.

He covered all of fifty yards before the next shooters blocked his path. These were mercs, running low and fast through the darkness, homing on the sound of the initial gunshot to locate its source. Johnny saw two of them, hoping he hadn't missed any. He shouldered the MP-5, sighting quickly on the closer of the two, and fired for effect.

The point man may have seen it coming; he seemed to flinch and shy away, taking the first round in his shoulder and rolling aside as the others scorched empty air. It was a painful, possibly debilitating wound, but he hit the ground breathing when he should've been stone dead.

Johnny swung toward his second target, wasting no time, but the shooter had dropped to the ground as soon as his comrade was hit. That made it two down but still breathing.

Johnny shifted, staying low, and found shelter behind a stout oak as one of the mercs returned fire. The shooter hadn't marked his shift, and the burst of fire cut through greenery where he'd been standing seconds earlier. Johnny saw the muzzle-flash and sighted on it, two bursts close together in a variation on the classic double-tap, but Johnny couldn't tell if he'd been lucky. Holding steady on the sights to scan for movement, he was barely quick enough to save himself when one of his opponents returned fire, knocking chips and splinters from the trunk that shielded him.

He had their general position in his mind's eye as he palmed a frag grenade and hooked the pin with his thumb, prying it free. Johnny gauged the distance to his target, calculated time in flight and judged the risk of being hit when he exposed himself to make the pitch.

He found the risk acceptable and started counting down the numbers.

One.

Johnny released the grenade's safety spoon and heard the snap of its six-second chemical fuse.

Two.

He drew back his arm for the throw, muscles clenching in his thighs.

Three.

A step around the oak, and Johnny made the toss, retreating even as twin muzzle-flashes winked from the shadows in front of him.

Four.

Regaining his grip on the MP-5, he crouched and waited for the blast.

Five…six…

The detonation, though expected, made him wince—but it was not about to slow him down. Johnny burst from cover in a rush, sweeping the field for targets, finger tensing on his weapon's trigger as he closed the gap between himself and sudden death.

LUIS GONZALES scowled and watched the whole thing go to shit. One of the men seated behind him in the El Dorado muttered, "Another fucking mess they got."

Gonzales couldn't argue that point, but his shooter had it wrong in one sense, anyhow. It was his mess, as much as anyone's, though he had no part in creating it and would've been delighted to drive off and let the crazy bastards kill one another.

But it wasn't up to him.

Any sense of independence he'd been feeling lately in Miami had been throttled by a phone call from Pablo Aznar.

Aznar was the voice of Hector Santiago, and his hard right hand as well.

Gonzales had a choice. He could either help Aznar teach a lesson this night, or else he could become the object lesson for others tomorrow.

And that, in reality, was no choice at all.

The message from Cali was simple: Keep an eye on Maxwell Reed and help out as needed if some crazy gringos showed up to waste him. Gonzales cared nothing for the islander or his politics, but Mr. Santiago wanted him alive, and that made Reed's survival a matter of pressing concern to Gonzales.

He'd been hoping the long night would pass without incident, dozing in his seat while the others kept watch, but then the sounds of combat had jarred him awake.

What to do?

They could stand by and wait for the cops to arrive, which wouldn't take long in this tight-ass ritzy neighborhood, but Reed might be killed while they sat on the street and listened to the battle from a distance. Gonzales didn't need to guess how Mr. Santiago would react to that; he knew the answer only too well. Danger of imminent arrest meant nothing when orders had been given. Death was the only acceptable excuse for failure—and the only refuge for those who disappointed the cartel.

Gonzales lifted the Uzi that lay between his feet and flicked off the safety. "Come on," he said.

"We have to go in there?" one of the back-seat shooters asked him.

"That, or tell Mr. Aznar you were afraid," Gonzales said.

There were no further protests, only the sharp metallic click-clack of automatic weapons being primed. Gonzales stepped out of the Cadillac and shut the door behind him, riotous gunfire muffling the sound as it closed. He crossed the street and knew without looking back that the others would follow. They feared him, and rightly so, but above all else they feared the wrath of Cali, perfect and immutable.

Gonzales cursed himself for bringing only four men, but it was too late to call for reinforcements now. They would do what they could and to hell with the rest. Colombians were known for their ferocity in battle. With any luck, it might be enough.

They reached the gate that barred Reed's driveway. Standing underneath the floodlights there, a black man dressed in a baggy shirt and trousers aimed a handgun at them, through the wrought-iron bars. He demanded to know what they wanted.

"We've come here to save your ass," Gonzales answered him. "Now open up the fucking gate!"

KEELY ROSS SURPRISED her adversaries. Stepping from the shadow of a Japanese maple, she raked the trio from behind with a burst of autofire that scythed across their skirmish line from left to right. Two of the three sprawled facedown on the grass, twitching. The third spun like a dervish, took a hit or two and went down on his side. But he was staring back at her, a weapon in his big hands angling toward her face.

She fired again to finish him, but ducking spoiled her aim. The wasted bullets sizzled high and wide above her target, while his own first shot was true enough to pluck at Ross's sleeve. It traced a razor line of fire across her bicep, close enough to let her know that half an inch would have meant a shattered humerus, leaving her arm flapping useless at her side.

She let the duck become a dive, plunging headlong to earth as her wounded enemy kept firing, the muzzle of his weapon leaping erratically. Ross fired and fired, shell casings pumping from the MP-5's ejection port, and somewhere in the midst of it she saw a number of her rounds strike flesh.

The human target shivered, dying, his weapon bucking free of numb and useless hands. Ross, winded by her fall, scanned the bodies and pushed up to all fours only when she was certain they were down for good.

But she was wrong.

The middle man, second to fall, lurched up on his hands and knees as she was rising. Like a wounded animal, he shook his head and snarled at the resulting pain. Ross didn't know if he was wearing Kevlar, or if she had simply missed all vital organs when she shot him in the back. Whatever, he was reaching for the rifle he'd dropped when he fell. He'd reached it, fingers scrabbling at the pistol grip, when Ross stepped up behind him, on his right, and shot him in the head at point-blank range.

There were tears in her eyes, a mixture of rage and revulsion she couldn't contain, but Ross left them to dry on their own. She had more work to do, and logic told her she hadn't seen the worst of it yet.

Which way to go?

Their target was the house, and since she had no solid reason to believe her comrades had been neutralized, Ross stayed the course. She had some thirty yards to go before she cleared the trees, another thirty-plus to reach the patio and swimming pool.

Her headset was silent, and Ross resisted the temptation to ask her companions if they were still alive. She was afraid of what would happen, how she might react, if she called out their names and neither man responded.

Grim-faced, she pushed on toward the house.

BOLAN RECOGNIZED the men spilling out of the house through a side door, weapons in hand as they moved toward their waiting crew wagons, parked three abreast. He didn't know their names but there was no mistaking the type. Shiny suits, slicked-back hair; facial expressions stuck somewhere between nervous and nasty. He'd hunted their kind long enough to know them by sight.

They were Mafia.

Bolan broke into a jog, closing the gap between them in the darkness, before the point men had a chance to see him coming. They were focused on the cars, presumably intent on hauling ass away from the estate that had become a battleground.

Too late.

Still running full-tilt, Bolan primed a grenade and hurled it downrange. He saw it strike the grass and wobble underneath the front end of the middle car. Diving, he hit the deck and waited for the thunder, sighting down the barrel of his MP-5.

The explosion was muffled, sandwiched between the earth and several tons of prime Detroit steel. It did the job anyway, lifting the crew wagon's nose a couple of feet off the ground while flames licked around the engine compartment and found the fuel line. It wouldn't have damaged a real armored car, but Joey DeMitri had been cutting corners and it showed. The limo went to hell in seconds flat, spewing streamers of fire across the yard and the vehicles parked close on either side.

Bolan was watching the men, at least twenty in number, as they recoiled from the spreading fire. Those were long odds against him, but he didn't hesitate. Surprise was a weapon as deadly as shrapnel or flame.

He raked the clutch of milling gangsters with a stream of Parabellum manglers, firing off two-thirds of a fresh 30-round magazine before he released the SMG's trigger. The slugs did their job, ripping flesh and bone, dropping men to the turf before they realized what was happening around them. Maybe half the shooters went down in that first blaze of fire, dead or wounded, leaving their companions blood-spattered and stunned.

Bolan knew his time was short before the men still on their feet recovered enough to seek targets. He switched to 3-round bursts and started taking down selected targets among the survivors, firing first at those who seemed to have their wits about them, blowing gaps in the ragged line while the men he bypassed were left gasping in shock.

One round left in the SMG's magazine, and Bolan used it on a shooter who had spotted him. The gunman's face was blood-flecked from the passing of a comrade, one eye squinting where the crimson droplets had smeared on lid and lashes, slowing him further. Bolan closed the other eye with his last 9 mm round, dropping the guy in his tracks and ditching the spent magazine instantly, feeding a fresh one into the MP-5's receiver as two more shooters saw him and called out warnings to their surviving comrades.

Some of the survivors opened fire as Bolan finished reloading, the rest breaking for cover while they had a chance to save themselves. Bolan cocked the MP-5 and went back to work, holding steady while the slugs swarmed overhead and brought the air to life with rattling, sizzling sounds.

He tracked across the killing field from right to left this time, short bursts for each of those who stood their ground, four men in all. The rest were off and running, some back toward the house, others seeking their refuge in the trees and shadows some way off.

Bolan went back to work.

WAYLON SPADE had no idea exactly what the hell was happening. He knew that Reed's mansion was under attack; that much was obvious. In terms of pinning down the individuals responsible and stopping them, however, Spade was literally groping in the dark.

And he was running out of time.

His first problem was the chaotic response of Reed's islanders to the initial gunshot. They were spooked by yesterday's events in Miami, the condition aggravated by reports of the previous slaughter in Louisiana. One stray shot was all it took to ignite a firestorm. His mercs were trying to control the panic, but they were outnumbered four or five to one by Reed's countrymen, and it took time to circulate, shaking the bastards back into some kind of order.

They might've passed one gunshot off as a backfire, someone passing on the street with a defective muffler, but this frantic action would have police on the way in nothing flat.

He had run to the spot where the first frag grenade exploded, finding two of the home team dead from a combination of gunshot wounds and shrapnel. There was no sign of their killer, other than a scattering of 9 mm Parabellum brass on the ground some distance from the corpses.

Spade was still fuming over that, looking for targets to absorb his rage, when another explosion rocked the night. This one was closer to the house, and that meant trouble.

Spade doubled back toward the house, running at top speed, clutching his MP-5 K in a death grip. Twice he spotted members of his team along the way, three men in all, and called them to him without breaking stride.

He knew they were in trouble when he saw the burning cars. They were Alessio's crew wagons, and the corpses scattered around the smoking vehicles were Alessio's men—or most of them, at any rate.

"They're still here," he told the mercs. "We need at least one prisoner alive and talking. Bag one any way you can and be prepared to haul ass out of here. It won't be long before we're eyeball deep in badges."

His men acknowledged the command with jerky nods, and they were starting to disperse when the west wing of Reed's house exploded, raining glass, plaster and shards of smoking lumber down on Wayland Spade.

Bolan hadn't really meant to set the house on fire. He'd been pursuing stragglers from the group of men he'd gunned down near the burning cars, when a pair of riflemen opened up on him from a side door of Maxwell Reed's mansion. They were hasty, letting their rifles kick too high to score a kill in full-auto mode, and Bolan had driven them back under cover with fire from his SMG.

The door beckoned, still open, revealing a bright slice of kitchen beyond, and he'd decided that there'd never be a better time to check the house and find out if Reed was still inside. The two defenders hadn't fled beyond the kitchen, though, and they were ready to prevent his passing through that way while they survived.

The trick was to make sure they didn't stay alive.

Trading fire with entrenched defenders was a losing game, especially when sirens would be screaming down the street outside Reed's fortress any moment. Bolan armed another of his frag grenades, maneuvered into range, and pitched it through the open doorway to the room beyond.

He never understood exactly what transpired within the next few seconds. Possibly a bullet had already clipped the stove's gas line, or shrapnel may have done the job when the grenade exploded. For all he knew, Reed's soldiers may have stored munitions in the pantry with the canned goods and cleansers. Some people are just that stupid.

Whatever the cause, his grenade's detonation was followed instantly by a second, more powerful explosion. It started in the kitchen and ripped through the west wing of the house, blowing out windows and buckling walls, gutting the ground floor and dropping the second floor to fill a sudden void below. The blast left fire in its wake, swiftly spreading to undamaged parts of the house.

Bolan took for granted that the kitchen riflemen were dead, and so was any hope of entering the house from that direction. As to seeking Maxwell Reed, Bolan surmised that he'd do better watching exits now, rather than looking for a way to prowl inside the blasted hulk while it burned down around him.

Sirens sounded in the distance. Bolan was moving toward the mansion's broad front porch when Keely Ross spoke to him from the night.

"Heads-up," her small voice said. "I hope I'm not alone out here."

"I hear you," Johnny answered, with a crackle of small-arms fire in the background.

"I copy," Bolan added, still moving.

"We've got police coming," Ross warned them. "Any sign of Reed?"

"Not yet," Johnny said.

"Nothing here," Bolan added.

"How much longer are we giving it?" Ross asked.

Johnny answered with a question of his own. "Five minutes?"

"Five it is," Bolan replied.

A lot could happen in five minutes, possibly too much. If Maxwell Reed was still invisible, they'd have to face the fact he might be dead, or that he may have flown the coop before they had arrived. In either case, they would gain nothing by remaining at the scene to face Miami's finest.

It was nearly time to cut and run—but not just yet.

Bolan still had one card to play, and it could make a world of difference in the killing game.

LUIS GONZALES SAW the house on fire and knew they were too late to save whoever or whatever was inside it. It had been a stupid notion from the start, but he was bound to try if Aznar and Santiago decreed it.

Gonzales heard the sirens, standing in the middle of Maxwell Reed's driveway with an Uzi clutched to his chest and no one to kill.

The best Gonzales could do, in the circumstances, was to keep his team intact and get away from there before the cops piled out of their squad cars with weapons drawn, faces carved into masks of rage and contempt.

"Vamanos!" he snapped at the others. "We're getting out of here."

They turned back to the street and their waiting car. The wrought-iron gate stood open and unguarded, since Gonzales had spooked the lone sentry into flight. They cleared it and were almost to the curb, ready to cross the two-lane residential blacktop, when the first police car screamed into view, its driver laying on the brakes and smoking tires at the sight of five armed Colombians crossing the street.

That does it, Gonzales thought. We're in the shit now.

He didn't wait for the doors on the squad car to open. Instead of barking orders at his men, Gonzales led them by example, leveling his Uzi from the hip and unleashing a stream of automatic fire from twenty feet. His Parabellum rounds cracked windshield glass, glanced off bright chrome and blew apart the flashing colored lights atop the cruiser's roof.

Before the men around Gonzales could react, more police cars were screeching to a halt in the street, spilling uniformed men and women left and right. The officers crouched behind open doors, angling their pistols and shotguns toward Gonzales and his men.

Gonzales shouted orders.

His men opened fire in unison, bullets flaying the street. Cops were falling, but most of them returned fire with a vengeance, blasting away at their targets from a range that made it difficult to miss.

Gonzales took a hit above his belt line, feeling as if a heavyweight boxer had punched him with a loaded glove. His legs betrayed him, buckling, and he crumpled to the pavement. Warm blood splashed his tailored linen slacks.

Gonzales kept his grip on the Uzi, returning fire through the waves of mortal agony. He had never learned how to quit once the battle was joined. A moment later his magazine was empty, but he fumbled in his jacket pocket, bloody fingers slipping on the metal of another clip before he hauled it clear.

For just a moment, he was conscious of the bodies sprawled around him, recognizing that he was alone. One of the cops called for him to surrender, but he answered with a Spanish curse. Gonzales struggled to his knees, pointing his weapon at the nearest cruiser and its occupants.

The firing squad in blue cut loose.

AT LAST, Wayland Spade had his target. Dressed in black, with his face painted to match, the man was dueling with two of Reed's men when Spade first caught a glimpse of him.

Spade nearly tried to drop him on the spot, but he was

more than sixty yards away and didn't trust the MP-5 K's reach at that range. It would kill all right, if he could score a hit, but missing was the best way to announce his presence while allowing his adversary a chance to hit back.

Instead of firing, then, Spade ran. He made a beeline for the man in black, closing the gap between them in a sprint. It wasn't quiet, but there was enough noise still around the house and grounds to cover something simple like a running man.

Or so he hoped.

Spade's target was moving around the east end of the house, or what remained of it, scanning the smoky darkness in search of defenders. If the approaching sirens bothered him, the stranger didn't let it show—but they were working on Spade's nerves. He heard the first of several cruisers squeal to a halt in the street out front, and when the shooting started he wondered if Reed's men were really dumb enough to fire on Miami PD.

Spade hoped not, but it stood to reason that the cops weren't shooting at one another.

He concentrated on his mark, picking up speed as he trailed the black-clad man around toward the front porch of Reed's residence. Any second now, and he'd be close enough to try a killing shot.

The lone intruder slowed. Spade moved up behind him, not at all concerned about shooting his quarry in the back. Chivalry was for movies and long-dead cowboys, the furthest thing from his mind in a fight.

He raised the machine pistol, aiming at his target from a range of thirty feet or less. Spade's finger curled around the trigger, taking up the slack. He held his breath—

And saw the shooter pivot like a gymnast, dropping to a crouch as he unloaded with his SMG, the muzzle flashes winking straight at Spade.

JOHNNY FIRED on instinct, before he'd made true target acquisition, trusting his skill and his weapon to take it from there. A short burst, no more than four or five rounds. He saw the target stagger, right leg folding to let him drop, but that didn't mean he'd scored a kill.

Kevlar could work wonders, for example, and the shooter might be waiting for him to advance so he could make the score at point-blank range.

He circled to the fallen shooter's left, keeping the downed man's firearm and his gun hand in view at all times. There might be other weapons Johnny couldn't see from where he stood, but the immediate threat was an MP-5 K machine pistol. Anything else would require sudden movement and grappling with clothes, a fatal delay when Johnny already had the man covered.

The last few paces, Johnny knew his adversary wasn't faking and there'd been no Kevlar. Blood was soaking through the gunman's shirt and nylon windbreaker, bright crimson from a lung shot. He was choking on it, bubbles forming on his lips when he exhaled, collapsing with a gargling sound when he inhaled.

How long before he stopped?

It took another beat or two, but Johnny recognized the blood-smeared face. He'd seen it scowling from a photo at their final briefing.

This was Waylon Spade.

He knelt beside the dying mercenary, close enough for Spade to use a knife if he'd remembered to put one up his sleeve, but Spade was preoccupied with dying at the moment. His eyes focused reluctantly when Johnny shook him by one shoulder. He seemed resentful, struggling feebly against the hand that turned him over on one side, clearing his airway.

"You're dying," Johnny told him. "It's over, and I need to find Maxwell Reed. Point me to him, and we can make this easier."

Spade's crimsoned lips pulled back into an eerie grimace-smile. "Y-y-you mi-missed him, a-a-ass—"

The curse was lost in ghastly choking sounds.

Outside, the screaming sirens had crescendoed and then died away. No matter how he sliced it, it was time to leave.

Johnny keyed the headset's microphone and told the night, "Reed's gone. We missed him. Time to bail."

"I copy," Ross replied.

Bolan answered him with a reluctant, "Roger that."

Johnny rose and ran north, toward the trees.

IT WAS ABOUT DAMN TIME. Police were at the gate, maybe inside the fence, and Keely Ross was in a hopeless situation if they caught her there. She knew Koontz wouldn't back her up on anything like this. She'd be expected to keep her mouth shut, to fall on her sword as it were, for the good of the agency.

Like hell.

She'd taken the risk upon herself, but Ross wasn't a quitter. She wasn't about to surrender while there were any alternatives on tap.

She ran as if grim Death were breathing down her neck, no great exaggeration from the sounds of combat still raging around Reed's estate. Police had joined the battle now, and that meant double trouble, since Ross knew she couldn't bring herself to return their fire if they spotted her.

At least she wouldn't be a sitting duck. Not even close.

Ross made it to the outer wall. She scaled it as she had in training, digging in with toes and fingertips between the cinder blocks, up and over. She expected cops to rush her when she landed on the grass outside, but they were nowhere to be seen.

Too much hot action at the gate, so far, for them to throw up a perimeter. She took advantage of the lapse and made her ducking, dodging way back to the Lincoln Town Car.

She was the first one there, but they all had keys, just in case someone fell by the wayside. That kind of precaution saved lives in a crunch.

Anytime, guys. No need to be stylishly late.

She slipped into the driver's seat and put her key in the ignition slot. She didn't start the engine, afraid that it would draw attention to her, even with the racket on the grounds.

The engine had been working when they got there; it would work all right next time she turned the key, without a test to calm her nerves.

Sit tight. Just wait.

JOHNNY WAS CROUCHING near the Lincoln, curbside, and Ross was in the driver's seat when Bolan stepped out of the shadows, joining them.

"You cut it close," Johnny said, sounding relieved.

"A couple of Reed's people wanted me to stick around," Bolan replied.

Ross waited until the two of them were seated, then she switched on the engine and pulled out from the curb, resisting the impulse to burn rubber in some melodramatic zero-to-seventy getaway ploy. They were safer just driving the limit, maybe a little over, like anyone out on the town. They had to lose the war paint as soon as possible, but there were tissues and cold cream in the car ready and waiting.

"How'd you know Reed split?" Bolan asked his brother.

"I got it straight from Wayland Spade."

"He wasn't conning you?" Ross asked. She drove with one

hand, smearing cold cream on her cheeks and forehead with the other.

Johnny shook his head. "He didn't have a con left in him. Trust me."

"So," Ross pressed, "where did they send him?"

"That, Spade couldn't say."

"Dammit!"

"We'll check with Washington when we get clear," Bolan said. "One of our sections may have something on the move."

"Could be." Ross did a decent job of masking any optimism.

"If they don't," Johnny remarked, "we'll need someone to squeeze."

"Maybe DeMitri's people," Ross suggested, "if they're not out of the loop."

"Or Reed's," Johnny added. "That's assuming we can track them down, after tonight."

"We'll find somebody, if it comes to that," the Executioner replied.

He watched patrol cars streaming past them in the opposite direction, colored lights ablaze and sirens keening. The cops were in a hurry, too excited by the shooting call to even register the Lincoln in their minds.

He ran a mental catalog of what they'd left behind, at the crime scene. Some footprints. Scuffs and scratches where they'd scaled the wall at different places. Lots of brass they'd never handled without latex gloves. Grenade shrapnel and residue. Bullets that would identify their weapons, if and when the guns were ever found for a comparison.

And bodies.

How many?

Bolan wasn't sure. There'd been no time for counting in the heat of battle, but he knew they hadn't killed enough. Not yet.

The men behind the plot were still alive and in the wind. Worse yet, he didn't know all of their names yet.

Hell, he couldn't even say with any certainty what they were plotting.

There were too many unanswered questions, and he couldn't let it go until they were resolved. Once Bolan had the information he required, he'd also have a final list of targets, and the bloodshed would begin in earnest.

Everything they'd done so far had simply been a prelude to the main event, but it was coming. Bolan felt it in his gut.

It was the kind of situation Bolan understood.

He didn't have to like it. All he had to do was stay alive and play the game out to its end.

**13**

*Key West, Florida*

"You're sure he's dead?" Tripp frowned around the words. "There's no mistake?"

"We ran his prints," the gruff voice said. "It's Spade, all right."

Tripp's contact was a sergeant with the state police who lived beyond his means to satisfy a second wife twelve years his junior, trading tips and favors in return for cash the tax man couldn't trace. This time around he had verified that Wayland Spade was one of those cut down in the firefight at Maxwell Reed's estate.

"Okay," he said. "Is there any ID on the others?"

"You want the whole list?"

"How long is it?" Tripp asked. The early media reports had been vague, referring to a major loss of life without specific figures.

"Forty-seven, counting Spade and the five Colombians."

Jesus Christ. "What Colombians?"

"We've only got names on a couple of those," the sergeant replied. "They were out in the street when the first squad cars got there. One of them started shooting, capped a couple of cops. The boys took them down."

Colombians. He'd have to think about that when he had a spare moment. "Forget them and the cops," he said. "Just the others."

"It's your dime."

The sergeant began reading names from a more-or-less alphabetical list. Tripp recognized four of his mercs and a couple of Reed's entourage. Danny Alessio was on the list, together with most of the crew he'd brought in to assist. That meant another vacancy at the top of the DeMitri Family, but that wasn't Tripp's problem.

When the sergeant finally finished reading, Tripp asked him, "Is there anyone on there who doesn't belong?"

"Meaning what?"

"Say Caucasians who weren't on the staff, for example. Maybe paramilitary types?"

"No whites except security people and Alessio's goombahs."

"Okay, then."

"That's it?"

"All I need," Tripp replied. "You'll be paid through the usual channels."

Spade was replaceable, of course. Tripp had a man in mind for the job already, but it was still a bit of a shock to lose him that way, gunned down on a routine security assignment. Then again, nothing had been routine since the woman showed up on Bayou LaFourche.

Tripp needed to find out who she was, what her connections were, and how she'd managed to throw such a huge fucking wrench in the works. More importantly, he had to find out where she was, along with any sidekicks linked to the attacks on his men and Reed's soldiers. Find out and eliminate the troublemakers before they gave him any more grief.

Or maybe the bastards could just spin their wheels for a while, now that Tripp was taking the action offshore. What were the odds that the shooters would follow the game down to Panama? How would they even know the field of play had shifted?

Tripp was packed and ready to go. One holdover from his military days was a facility for living out of duffel bags. He didn't mind at all—preferred it, in fact, to the settled life of mortgages and matching furniture.

Maybe, when he was the commander of the military forces on Isla de Victoria, Tripp would consider settling down.

Maybe not.

Meanwhile, he had a war to win, and he was running out of time.

MAXWELL REED WAS HAPPY to be airborne that morning, despite the early hour. He had watched the sun rise over the Bahamas, bound for a refueling stop at Santo Domingo. It was good to be moving again, shaking off the inertia of rest.

Pursuing his destiny.

The day of reckoning had been a long time coming, and it still lay just beyond his reach. But it was growing closer now. Reed felt it in his bones.

The setbacks in Louisiana and Miami didn't matter. Neither did the compromises he'd been forced to make along the way, to realize his vision of ultimate triumph. Of course there'd been bargains, agreements, concessions. What statesman had ever existed without them?

It had been years since Reed set foot in Panama. The Chinese hadn't been a factor then, but they were ubiquitous now. So much the better, then, that he had courted their favor. He envisioned the new Isla de Victoria as a truly cosmopolitan nation, serving the world at large and being well served in return. There would be naysayers, of course. Reed never doubted that. The test of statesmanship lay in the means by which he dealt with opposition, the effectiveness of his response.

Gone were the days when a tyrannical regime in Washington could easily afford to send U.S. Marines and blot out a progressive government over some philosophical differences. Tax laws and banking regulations were nothing, in the scheme of things. Once Reed's administration was established, he expected American industrialists and politicians to take full advantage of the services his government would offer.

And why not?

They hid their fortunes in the Cayman Islands now, in Switzerland and Liechtenstein. When times were hard, they hid themselves in Costa Rica, Portugal, South Africa. Everyone was security conscious, with ruinous taxation and government snooping the cold rule of thumb. Reed knew what it meant to be hunted. His sympathies naturally lay with the prey.

All his life, it seemed, he had been swimming hard against the tide. A rebel and the son of rebels in his native land, he had been jailed and beaten, nearly killed on more than one occasion, spared by the all-knowing hand of providence. It was his destiny to liberate the island of his birth. Who would dare to criticize his choice when he established free schools for his people, when he offered health care, guaranteed employment and an end to pervasive poverty?

Reed didn't care if Washington reviled his friends, the men who had supported him when no one else in Britain or America cared enough to cast their lot with the underdog. If some of them were also rebels, if they flouted laws that seemed to exist primarily for the benefit of corrupt U.S. and British officials, so what?

Maxwell Reed knew exactly who—and what—his bene-factors were. And he had welcomed them into the fold be-cause he needed them, their money and their strength, to make his dreams come true.

It was that simple, that complex.

And winging south across the blue Caribbean, Reed man-aged to convince himself that there was nothing anyone could do to stop him.

He was on his way.

His destiny was almost close enough to touch.

*Panama City*

SUN ZU-WANG was not pleased to be chosen for the role of a glorified baby-sitter, but he knew from experience that progress sometimes entailed distasteful duties. He would guard Maxwell Reed and cater to the politician's needs—up to a point—but he would not allow Reed to interfere with the operations of his empire in the making.

Reed was merely a tool, after all. His longevity and his utility were inextricably linked. If Reed was no longer use-ful—or, if he became an obstacle to progress—he would be eliminated with a nod to one of Sun's triad lieutenants.

No man was indispensable. No revolution triumphed with-out loss.

Maxwell Reed was a tool to help Sun achieve his ultimate goal of personal, political and financial invulnerability. He longed to be untouchable, effectively beyond the reach of en-emies, secure against all threats except the immutable, relent-less march of time.

He sipped his third martini of the day while waiting in a

private section of the airport's VIP lounge, glancing occasionally at his $30,000 Rolex wristwatch. An extravagant watch was no guarantee against wasting precious time, but Sun Zu-Wang was ever vigilant, guarding against his own worst impulses, enforcing a brand of self-discipline few men ever achieve outside of military service or a monastery.

Sun was not a monk, to be sure, but he was a warrior of sorts. Instead of cause or country, though, his primary loyalty was to himself, and after that to the triad he commanded.

Priorities were everything.

Reed's flight had been five minutes late departing from Miami, another fifteen minutes leaving Nassau, but it still somehow managed to touch down on time. His soldiers surrounded him as Sun left the VIP lounge, moving to meet his guest at the arrival gate. Strangely, his mind chose that moment to produce an image from an old American TV show. It was Fantasy Island, Ricardo Montalban standing on a tropical veranda with a dwarf at his side, commanding his lackeys to be cheerful.

Smiles, everyone. Smiles!

Sun smiled and waited for his puppet to deplane.

*Washington, D.C.*

HAL BROGNOLA SAT and waited for the telephone to ring. Even so, the telephone's shrill signal nearly made Brognola jump. He grabbed the receiver before it could sound off again.

"Brognola," he said by way of salutation.

"Anything new on our guy?" Bolan asked.

Brognola was relieved to have the answer. "Panama," he said. "I just confirmed it. He caught a charter out of Miami ninety minutes or so before your party in Fort Lauderdale. You just missed him."

Bolan, his tone mixing weariness with suspicion asked, "Do you think he was tipped?"

Brognola answered with a question of his own. "Who knew your plans?"

"Only the three of us."

"Meaning one suspect, right?"

Bolan considered it, a silent moment stretching out between them. "No," he said at last. "She didn't have the opportunity."

"Okay. Why would she tip him, anyway?"

"You're right. Call it coincidence. Tripp recognized a weak spot and took care of it."

"You got his number two, though," Brognola replied. "If it matters. Major heat's coming down on the DeMitri Family, or what's left of it. Whatever Reed and Tripp were planning, they just lost a sponsor."

"Something tells me they've got more on tap. Why Panama?"

"We don't have any fix on that so far," Brognola admitted. "The Bureau's supposed to have one of its people at the airport, watching whoever meets the flight. We'll know as soon as they do, more or less."

Bolan's mind was already free-wheeling. "DeMitri won't have anyone significant in Panama," he said. "Maybe a jobber for narcotics shipments, but there won't be any troops. Who's big in Panama right now?"

They both knew the answer to that one, but Brognola played the game. "Besides the president and military?" he replied. "Chinese."

"And given Reed's track record for recruiting allies in the States, whose likely to back him in Panama City?"

Brognola didn't mind the questions. They were nearly done, and nowhere close to twenty. "The triads," he answered dutifully.

"No problem for that crew to cover him," Bolan said.

"None that I can see from here."

"They'll be on guard, though."

"Maybe not so much," Brognola said. "They have a thousand miles between them and the last known trouble spot. Add that to five or six years digging in and buying allies in the government. It breeds self-confidence."

"Maybe too much," Bolan replied.

"I take it you'll be needing transportation, then?"

"I'm looking at the charter route," Bolan said, "since the military's not an option."

He was right on that score. Since the pullout, back in 1999, the closest U.S. military base to Panama was located in Puerto Rico. Charter flights weren't as secure, but with some skilled finagling and sufficient ready cash on hand, they could bypass most difficulties with a Third World customs service.

"I'll have backup on standby, just in case," Brognola said.

"It couldn't hurt," Bolan replied. "I'll touch base from the other end."

Brognola cradled the receiver as a Japanese proverb came out of nowhere, asserting itself in his mind. It was a haiku or some such, he thought. The message: It is better to travel hopefully than to arrive.

And wasn't that the bloody awful truth?

*St. Petersburg, Russia*

THE LINE WAS crystal clear for once, a novelty for conference calls in Semyon Borodin's experience. Usually by the time he had five people on the telephone and scramblers engaged for security, he was accustomed to static that made conversation a struggle. This time, at least, it seemed that they had caught a lucky break.

And none too soon, Borodin thought. Fortune had not exactly smiled on them of late.

"You think the situation in America can be resolved?" he asked.

"I'd say it is resolved," came the reply from Garrett Tripp. "We've cut our losses, pulled up stakes and gotten the hell out of Dodge. Whoever's been dogging us the past few days, they're fresh out of targets."

"You mean to say," Kenji Tanaka interjected, velvet-voiced, "that the targets have been moved. They still exist, as such."

"We've taken Reed out of harm's way," Tripp said. "De-Mitri and Ruggero are history, unfortunately. We'll have to do without them, but I don't foresee a problem there. If someone wants to pick over their bones in Miami or New Orleans, it makes a good diversion for the rest of us."

"I might feel more confident," Dante Ambrosio said, "if you knew the names of those responsible for killing my amici. It's an oversight that we could come to regret.

"I'm working on it," Tripp assured his sponsors. "As soon as something breaks, you'll know about it."

"And you will resolve the situation?" Ambrosio prodded.

"Of course, sir."

Borodin had to smile as the exchange played out. He knew all about the estrangement between the old-line Sicilian Mafiosi and their transplanted cronies in America. The two factions managed to collaborate from time to time, on major drug deals and the like, but they were worlds apart in terms of attitude, regarding each other as virtual strangers.

It was a weakness Borodin had once considered trying to exploit, but that plan would have to be shelved, now that the U.S. end of the plan was effectively crushed.

"To remain with this subject a moment longer," Borodin

said, "have you investigated the possibility of official involvement in the recent incidents?"

"Official?" The term seemed foreign to Tripp. "You mean Washington?"

"Or whoever." Geography meant less to Borodin than the strength and cunning of enemies who assailed him.

Tripp sounded confident as he replied, "The U.S. authorities don't play this way. Thirty years ago, maybe, before Nixon got his fingers burned on Watergate and the Allende thing, in Chile. Today they've got congressional oversight, they're paranoid about potential litigation, and the budget's well into red ink."

"I hope you're right," the Russian said.

"You're paying me to know these things," Tripp answered him.

"We're paying you to make this operation run like a well-oiled machine," Borodin replied. "Instead, it's on the verge of breaking down. Self-confidence may be an admirable quality, but it can also be misplaced."

"I've got it covered, gentlemen. Trust me."

It did not escape Borodin's notice that Tripp replied to the group at large, rather than speaking to him directly. The Russian frowned as he answered. "Trust has a price, Mr. Tripp. It must be earned, of course, but it must also be maintained. If it should fail at any point, because of poor performance… Well, you see the problem, yes?"

"We've definitely hit a snag," Tripp said. "I obviously can't deny it. But the problem's been contained, and I'll eliminate the source as soon as possible."

"And what if you're mistaken?" Hector Santiago asked, the first time he had spoken up from Cali since their salutations were completed. "What if this turns out to be some kind of U.S. operation after all?"

"I'll deal with it in any case," Tripp said. "They've killed my people. That requires some payback, gentlemen. Feds aren't immune. They're not about to get away with it."

"I sympathize," said the Colombian. Borodin knew that Santiago had eliminated troublesome officials on the home front, when the need arose. "But in the present atmosphere, perhaps retaliation isn't wise?"

"Leave that to me," Tripp said. "Whatever action I decide to take, you have my word the operation won't be jeopardized."

"And how would you achieve this miracle?" Kenji Tanaka asked.

"They'll look to those who have a grudge, when they start hunting suspects. Let DeMitri and Ruggero take the heat. It can't make any difference to them now."

Borodin smiled at that, but he couldn't resist dropping another stone into the pond. "Where is our friend from Panama tonight? I miss his insight, when we have such weighty problems to discuss."

"He's hosting our associate," Tripp answered. "You're at liberty, of course, to call him anytime you wish."

"Perhaps I will," the Russian said. "We don't want any more surprises, if the enemy you can't seem to identify should follow Reed from Florida."

"I'll be coordinating the security in Panama," Tripp said. "If anyone wants to contribute reinforcements—with Mr. Sun's blessing, that is—my men can always use the extra help."

"I'm sure we'll keep it in mind," Borodin said. "Meanwhile, if there's nothing else to discuss...? Nothing at all? Until the next time, then."

Reinforcements? he thought, as the line went dead in his hand. Perhaps observers was a better way to go, for now. Of course, they would be armed observers. What else? Borodin wouldn't send the lowliest member of his Family into a combat zone without some means of defending himself.

"Nicolai!" he called out to Yurochka, waiting in the anteroom next door. "Get half a dozen men together, right away. I feel the need for an inspection tour."

*Miami*

"PANAMA CITY?" Keely Ross looked confused. "Why on earth would he go to Panama City?"

"That's the question," Bolan replied. "The Bahamas and Jamaica are closer to Isla de Victoria, but that could be a problem in itself, for Reed."

"If he's not ready for the final push," Johnny said. "Whereas Panama would put him out of reach from Grover Halsey's people, and he may have friendlies waiting for him."

"Friendlies?" Ross still hadn't glimpsed the broad strokes.

"Chinese friends," Bolan suggested.

Ross blinked twice before she answered, "You mean Red Chinese?"

"I don't think anybody calls them that these days," Johnny replied.

He turned to face Bolan. "And I don't think that's who you've got in mind."

"Not quite."

"Triads," Johnny stated.

"More likely," the Executioner said. "It fits with Reed using DeMitri and Ruggero—or with them using him."

"A front man," Ross said.

"It stands to reason," Bolan answered, "when you think about it. He was hooked up with the Mob stateside, and they have their connections overseas. It's a natural link."

"And what if you're wrong?" Ross asked.

"It won't matter. Even if Reed doesn't have a working treaty with the Triads, he can't very well pitch camp in their backyard without paying his respects. At the very least they'll know where to find him."

"And you think they'll just tell you?"

"If I'm persuasive enough." Bolan left it at that.

"Okay," Ross said. "When do we leave?"

"We haven't decided who's going, yet," Bolan reminded her.

"That's right," Johnny added. "Panama's not exactly the Homeland."

Ross kept her gaze steady, facing each of them in turn across the table. "You think I'd miss the main event?" she asked. "I'm in this thing for the long haul, guys."

"No problem with jurisdictional issues?" Bolan asked.

"You're kidding me, right?" Her smile was strained, but hanging in there. "Have we done anything yet that falls within legitimate federal jurisdiction? Even one little thing?"

"This is different," Bolan reminded her. "Your people have no brief to operate outside the country, as I understand it. That's CIA territory, or maybe some part of the FBI's legal attaché network with the various embassies. Your team's on defense, as in working the home front."

"What's this? You never heard the old saying that the best defense is a good offense? Forget about it, gentlemen. I'm in." Ross was adamant.

"Just like that?" Johnny pressed. "What happens if the opposition bags you out of bounds, or you get busted?"

"The same thing that would've happened to me here," she answered without hesitation. "My people hang me out to dry and cook the books to make it seem like I never existed."

"Nice crowd," Johnny said.

"They're playing for keeps, just like you," she replied. "Just like me."

"In that case," Bolan said, "we need to get moving. Reed already has a head start, and I'm tired of playing catch-up."

A moment later they were on their feet and scrambling to pack their bags. Bolan knew their destination, but he couldn't say what would be waiting for them on arrival. He would simply have to wait and see.

So far, he had two elusive targets, one shaky ally and an unknown cast of characters standing by to receive them in Panama City. Taken all together, it told the Executioner he could rely on one thing.

They hadn't seen an end to killing yet.

In fact, the bloodshed had only begun.

\* \* \* \* \*

*Don't miss Executioner #309,*
FLAMES OF FURY, *Volume II*
*in the exciting ORG CRIME trilogy.*

# THE DESTROYER

## INDUSTRIAL EVOLUTION

### GUESS WHO'S COMING TO DINNER?

Take a couple of techno-geniuses on the wrong side of the law,
add a politician so corrupt his quest for the presidency is quite
promising and throw in a secret civilization of freaky-looking
subterranean dwellers who haven't seen the light of day in a
long time—it all adds up to one big pain for Remo.

*Book 2 of Reprise of the Machines*

*Available October 2004 at your favorite retail outlet.*

Stony Man is deployed against an armed
invasion on American soil...

# ROLLING
# THUNDER

The Basque Liberation Movement, a militant splinter cell of
Spain's notorious ETA terrorist group, has seized a state-of-the-
art new supertank equipped with nuclear firing capabilities. The
BLM has planned a devastating show of force at a NATO
conference in Barcelona. As Stony Man's cybernetics team
works feverishly to track the terrorists, the commandos of Able
Team and Phoenix Force hit the ground running. But a clever,
resourceful enemy remains one step ahead, in a race against
the odds getting worse by the minute....

# STONY MAN ®

*Available
August 2004
at your favorite
retail outlet.*

---

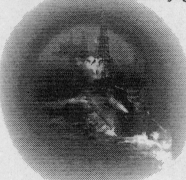